Losing Eddie

Losing Eddie

Deborah Joy Corey

Algonquin Books of Chapel Hill 1994

Published by
ALGONQUIN BOOKS OF CHAPEL HILL
Post Office Box 2225
Chapel Hill, North Carolina 27515-2225

a division of
WORKMAN PUBLISHING COMPANY, INC.
708 Broadway
New York, New York 10003

First Front Porch Paperback Edition, September 1994. Originally
published in hardcover by Algonquin Books of Chapel Hill in 1993.

Portions of this book have appeared, in slightly different
versions, in *The Agni Review, New Letters, Fiction, Story, The Windsor
Review, The Crescent Review, Best Stories from New Writers, The
Northcote Anthology, Three Genres of Fiction,* and *What If?*

LIBRARY OF CONGRESS CATALOGING-IN-PUBLICATION DATA
Corey, Deborah Joy, 1958–
Losing Eddie : a novel / by Deborah Joy Corey.
p. cm.
ISBN 1-56512-091-4
I. Title.
PR9199.3.C6525L67 1993
813'.54—dc20   92-40009
                                                                             CIP

2 4 6 8 10 9 7 5 3 1
First Printing

For my loving parents

I wish to thank The Canada Council and my editor, Shannon Ravenel, who generously teaches me.

Losing Eddie

Sister

I am sitting on the cool green grass when Sister comes rolling in the driveway. Her husband is driving their baby blue car. When the car stops, Sister grabs the car keys and throws them to the grass. "He's pounded my legs all the way here," she cries. Daddy comes down from the verandah. Sister is sobbing now and her babies are in the backseat with two brown bags of groceries, moving around in slow motion, rolling their fingers around their faces and breathing tiny spots of steam on the windows. Sister is still crying and I—with my good eye for shiny objects—find the keys and carry them back, using my index finger as a hook for the silver ring.

Daddy is talking to Sister's husband like nothing ever happened. Talking about the heat and the dry dusty air. I rest my chin on the open window and look down at Sister's lap; she is in a thin cotton dress and sure enough, all along her knee, round bruises have bunched themselves together like a cluster of old grapes.

The gravel driveway snaps under my flip-flops. I reach in front of Sister and dangle the keys like bells between her and her man. He grabs those keys and stares at Sister like she is a moving dart board and he is intent on making his point. I move away. Sister pushes open her door and pulls away from his grabbing hand. She runs across the lawn and her man jumps out of his car and follows her. He's taking giant steps behind Sister. He grabs her hair, which is short and has no give, he grabs it tight and drops her down on her back. His arm comes around in a half circle and his fist bashes into her face. I hear the wind push out of her. Daddy moves toward them, hollering, "Lydia, get out here."

Mama comes out of the house waving her white dish cloth in the air. "No," she screams, "not in my yard, not my girl." She runs to them, then stops and puts her hands on her hips. Mama's big and she makes Sister's man look small. "No," she says, firm.

Sister stands up and the blood spits out in a red waterfall. She covers her face and walks away, crooked. Daddy turns away to go into the house. His whole body droops like a rag. The girl baby starts to cry—wide opened-mouth cries—and everyone looks toward the car and they are all still and quiet on the sunburnt lawn. Then Sister's man makes his move. He runs to the car and starts it. The babies' faces look like melted masks against the windows. After their car pulls away, things are unusually close and quiet. We watch the car until all that is left is a swirling circle of dust over the road and Sister begins to cry, not a likely cry, but a cry like a moose's call, whiny and low.

In the night, I wake up because I feel crowded in my sleep. The day's heat is still trapped under my skin. I hear a train roll by two or three fields away and I listen until I can hear no more whistle. The silence blends in right along with my brother's wheezing. He sleeps in the hallway outside my door. I move to the window and play with the curl on the back of my neck. I push my face against the black screen to breathe a deeper breath of the clover smell moving on the wind and I think, Oh, Sister, I hope your face is okay. I hope your man learns to keep his temper down.

The fireflies cover the fields and heavens, flies and stars, all bright, first one, then the other, and I say, "Jesus, don't blame me for giving those keys back. But I don't want Sister living here, Jesus . . ." Brother wheezes louder. Wheezy Weasel, I call him when his chest gets heavy like this. His real name is Bucky. I go to check on him and he's fast asleep. His eyes cross furiously under his thin lids. I whisper his name. "Wheezy," I say, "get up quick, the whole world's on fire."

On Sunday Wheezy is sicker. His face has swollen red. Mama puts a mustard pack on his chest and head until his entire bed and body stain yellow. Mama hums him a hymn. She's humming, "Glory, glory, hallelujah!" She sings it over and over until my brother says, "Mama." He lifts his head and he says, "Mama, please no more."

Mama stops her singing right up quick and sends me away. I go down the back kitchen steps and out to where Daddy sits on the verandah. His face is long and brown kind of like an Indian's. He and Sister are talking about getting the babies back. Daddy is whittling a man's head out of a smooth piece of wood. There are tiny white shavings dropping between his legs. I go on out to the grass where I have worn a patch from sitting. I stay in that patch and watch the ghosts of dandelions blow through the air until Mama comes to get me for church.

Mama's shadow on the road is as big as the sun itself. She says Daddy will take care of things at home. She says my brother is feeling better. Mama's skin is white and thin like papier-mâché. I wonder if I will ever smell like her, clean and freshly brushed with dusting powder.

The touch of Mama's hand as I lie across her lap during the sermon comforts me. The preacher's voice is soft but the *Amens* echo around us like gunfire. "Amen," I say under my breath as I chew the thumbnail I have saved for this time alone with Mama. Even now, we're not really alone. I have to share Mama with her interest in what's being said.

When we get home, Sister and her babies are on the verandah with Daddy. You can tell by the way Sister is sitting that they are not discussing anything important. The babies stick their faces out through the slats of the railing and chew at the wood. Bucky is all covered with dried mustard sitting on the verandah step. His eyes in the sun are like green marbles. First thing Mama does is check his face for fever and pat the top of his head. I sit down beside him and twist my hair around my finger.

"Mama," Sister says, "Daddy went and got the babies back. He says there was nothing to it because their father was laid out cold on the couch." She says this very proud of Daddy, and Mama picks up one of the babies and looks into its face. Mama clicks her tongue and the baby smiles.

"Mama, I just gotta move back home. I can't take being scared all the time. I gotta get me and the babies out of that trailer before he kills us," Sister says. "Mama, can I come back home?"

Daddy stands up. He looks out over the lawn and taps the whittled man's head against the railing, then walks down to the old wellhouse, which is a storage space for his beer bottles. Daddy only drinks when things get too much for him, bills or my brother's wheezes. Sister sits up and watches Mama's face. She is as nervous as a tied dog.

"Mama," she snaps.

"You know we have nothing extra," Mama says and Sister starts up this long plea. Twisting her voice to match her words and saying she'll sleep on the floor, she won't eat much, she'll do anything just to get away from *him*. When I hear her talk about staying forever, I shrink into my body. Mama will be all tied up with Bucky and Sister and her babies, and Daddy will stay drunk, and I'll be nothing. I'll be the shriveled-up pea in the corner of the pod. Sister is like a long sticky flypaper fluttering in the wind and we are all the flies sticking to her troubles.

"What about your daddy?" Mama says. "He hasn't worked for a month and he says he doesn't know if he can make ends meet for all of us." She's bouncing the baby in her arms, up and down, swaying her hips like she's in a Hula Hoop.

"I'll do Tupperware parties and I'll pay rent," Sister says, making her face big-eyed like she already sees her great new life.

Mama takes the baby girl into the kitchen. The screen door bangs behind her. Sister picks up her other baby and balances him on her hip bone.

"Can I or can't I?" she asks. Mama stops and looks back at her. "You can stay in Eddie's room until he comes home."

Sister smiles and the worried lines go out of her face. I look at Mama, surprised to hear her mention our other brother. He has been in reform school for a long time and she has not said his name since the Mounties came by and said he'd been arrested.

The door of the wellhouse is slightly open. Standing near the crack, I can feel the cool from the darkness pushing out. There are empty brown bottles all along the walls and

it takes my eyes a minute to adjust without the sun. Daddy
is sitting in one corner with a piece of hay dangling from
his mouth. When he drinks, the hay stays in his mouth like
that, always. I sit down in the opposite corner beside a milk
can and roll an empty bottle in the palms of my hands.
"Well, I guess she's gonna stay," I say and Daddy just
watches me and drinks.

When he drinks, his Adam's apple bobs in and out like
a horse's heartbeat. I stare down at the musty floorboards.
Mama says Daddy drinks because his soul is troubled. She
also says if we could see our soul we'd see that it is in the
shape of wings. I believe her, because sometimes when I sit
on the lawn and stare out at the green mountain ridges that
surround our home place, I can feel my soul wanting to get
loose. I think it wants to know what's beyond those high
slopes. Daddy drinks a whole beer before he notices my
thumb is stuck in the top of the beer bottle and swelling
red from me tugging to get it out.

"What in hell?" Daddy staggers over toward me. He
grabs my arm and smashes the bottle against the old milk
can. The brown glass is sprinkled on top of my feet and I
struggle with the words in my throat, but they don't come

up. "Get out," he says, lifting me over the glass and out the door, which he slams behind me.

Daddy's anger is just the beginning of things with Sister being around. I wander around the yard and then out onto the road. I walk to the crossroads and take a turn toward the old folks' home that Mama calls heaven's waiting room. I stop at the black bridge, then sit and hang my feet out over the edge and stare down where the clear creek water rushes by like a jet. I can see the round rocks in the creek's bottom and wonder about my kazoo. I wonder if maybe it's hidden between those rocks and getting rusty. I dropped it over when I was thinking about a boy named Lenny Moore, the only boy in the whole third grade. He sits at the desk in front of me. He's jiggly and nervous, and he's always sending me notes about how he likes me and would like to kiss me someday. For a while I liked the notes and the thoughts I had of Lenny. I liked him a lot up until the day he wet his pants and his yellow water ran back under his chair toward my new white sneakers. It's hard to forget that and now the rest of the kids call him Leaky Moore, which keeps us both cringing and blushing.

The smell of the melting tar coming out around the

dark boards of the bridge is so strong you'd think it came in a black cloud. I swing my legs and forget about my thumb and Daddy and all the broken glass, but I still have a clear picture of Sister and her babies.

At the old folks' home, I crawl up on Mrs. Harris's bed and rest myself. Her room smells of plastic and fly repellent. She is wandering around the room touching all her things and saying, "I've got to get ready, I've got to get ready." Mama's been letting me come to visit Mrs. Harris all summer. She's always like this, not quite sure of where she belongs anymore. She says her old man sleeps up in the attic and bakes molasses cookies all day. She says the mosquitoes sneak in through her screen at night and bite her to death. I tell Mrs. Harris there is no screen on the window, but she just keeps on talking and smiling like I've never said a word. She takes some old crochet work out of a plastic bag and rubs her wrinkled fingers over it. I tell her about the gall of Sister and her babies moving right in with us, and she is so happy for me, having family and all. She puts the crochet work back in the bag, sniffing and trying to hide her sad joy. Before I leave, Mrs. Harris combs the snarls from my hair. While she combs it one hundred times I count the mosquito bites on her legs, which are really too many to count.

On the way home I find Daddy wading around in the creek. He is pushing his legs against the current and staring down through the water in a panic. I lean out over the water as far as I dare and I say, "Daddy, what are you doing?"

He looks up, his mouth is wilted and opened. He squints his eyes at me. He yells my name, the scream bouncing up under the bridge and back to the water. He rubs his face, then slaps at the current like he is disgusted, whispering my name, all worn out.

Daddy takes me home by the arm and his dripping pant legs make spots of mud on the dirt road. He hangs on to my arm like he's afraid I'll get away, like I'm some slippery trout and I know what he thinks. He's thinking that I might have been lying under the water, still, and in another world. He's thinking it over and over.

We are almost home and I can see Mama standing in the doorway wagging the flyswatter. Daddy keeps pulling me along and when we get to the verandah, Mama takes one big step toward us. She grabs my arm and I begin to circle around her trying to step over the flyswatter coming at my legs. "Don't *slap* you *slap* ever *slap* go *slap* away *slap* without *slap* telling *slap* us *slap* where *slap* you're *slap* going *SLAP SLAP.*" I run upstairs to my room and push my face in the feather pillow and for a long time I keep myself from looking at the red marks on my legs.

When Mama wakes me, the sun is gone. She takes me into her room where everyone except Daddy is sitting in the dark on the bed. They are all listening to the voice in the yard. Sister tells us her man is as drunk as a hoot. His words are running together like melting Jell-O. "Give me my babies, I want my kids back. Give 'em back or I'll shoot you all. I'll blow you all to kingdom come." Things get real still and you can feel the fear running through each of us as if we are all hanging on to the same electric fence. I can feel it pushing right out to the ends of my fingers. Bucky is shaking and just to watch him makes me shake. Sister wraps one arm around me. One time Daddy told us about a crazy man who went to a farmer's house and shot the farmer's whole family while they slept. Daddy said he'd never seen such a sight, all those bodies bled dry in their beds. I can see us all slumped over in this bed in a pool of blood, and right away everything I've told Mrs. Harris seems stupid.

We hear the screen door slam and Mama moves to the hall window. I go right behind her. Sister's man is sitting on the hood of his car with a bottle in one hand and a gun in the other. It's just like the gun Daddy uses to hunt deer. Sister's man is as loose as a Slinky. Daddy stands right in front of him. I close my eyes. "Give me the gun," Daddy says. "And then go home and get yourself sober." There is a tiny click and then stillness like the whole world has disappeared. I open my eyes and Sister's man points the gun right at Daddy's chest. Mama and I both pull our breath back through our mouths in a gasp. And Daddy reaches out and takes the gun in one clean sweep, smooth as honey, and Mama says, "Put the babies to bed."

Sister's man rolls himself into a ball. He says he has lost everything and starts to cry. He cries so hard and so loud that I think he is crying for all of us. It is like all of our hurts have snuck down inside of him and are now pouring out on top of his car in tears and wet noises.

Later, Daddy comes into my room and looks down at me and Sister's baby. The baby has its face shoved into the mattress and is sound asleep. Daddy says he wanted to make sure the bed is big enough for the baby and me. I say it is. He is just a tall dark shape in the middle of my room. He drops his hand down and I touch it. I feel the red metal of my kazoo hidden away in his palm. It is a lost treasure.

Daddy doesn't say anything, he just lets the kazoo go when he's sure I'm there to catch it and goes back to his room. I blow it once to see if it still works. The girl baby turns and snuggles up to my side. Her breath is sour and small and wispy. I listen to it go in and out of her like clockwork, then I imagine the flapping of wings all around me, in the night.

Woman Talk

Marilyn Morris and I are blood sisters. Yesterday she cut her finger with her daddy's razor and I punched mine open with a sewing needle. Her blood came quicker but I didn't have the nerve to slit myself. I just kept slowly poking the end of my finger until the needle finally went through. Marilyn said she never saw such a chicken as me, but I ignored her because I don't like to be bullied. We were sitting in the old car with no wheels behind her house. Marilyn was in the driver's seat and I was sitting where the wife always does. When we finally both got blood and rubbed our fingers together, Marilyn told me we were permanent friends. She said, "Nothing can come between us now."

Marilyn and I sit on the verandah and listen in through the screen to Mama's sewing machine speed up and then die down. Marilyn is sucking on her cut finger and I am chewing my last fingernail down to the quick. Mama is making clothes for Sister's babies because she says it's a shame for a child to have to wear the same thing three or four times a week. She says if you can, you should treat children like royalty because it was someone royal and divine who created them.

Mrs. Morris is in the rocking chair beside Mama. She brought her sewing basket and said she'd be more than happy to do the fine work and put on a bit of trim in a cross-stitch. The sound of Mrs. Morris rocking is slow and even. "Tired, tired, tired," she says to Mama. "I don't know what's wrong with me. I just don't seem to have any pep anymore."

"Have you seen Dr. Pearly?" Mama asks.

"Oh yes, a hundred times, but he always just tells me to get more rest. The funny thing is the more I rest the worse I feel." Mrs. Morris laughs. "I guess the cure has ended up being my curse."

The sewing machine keeps on humming. "It wouldn't be that you are having your change of life?" Mama's voice is just one notch above a whisper. Marilyn and I look at

16

each other and hold still to listen. Marilyn opens her eyes real wide like they are the part of her that hears.

"Well, I suppose anything's possible. It seems early, though, but then again, Mona up the road says she hasn't had a period in years."

I stop chewing my fingernail. "Period?"

Marilyn cups her hands around my ear and whispers, "Sanitary napkins."

I cover my mouth and laugh. Once we found a box of sanitary napkins in Mrs. Morris's closet and we each took one out to look at. I thought they were neck braces, but Marilyn knew better. She said they were for when a woman has blood come out.

"How do you know that?" I asked.

"I read it in that book of your sister's."

My bottom dresser drawer is full of Sister's things. She says they are keepsakes and she didn't want to take them with her when she got married. There is a box with odd earrings, a stack of movie star clippings, a rabbit's foot on a little chain, two pictures of her when she was a baby, and there used to be a thin book called *Now You Are a Woman*, until Marilyn got it from me. It has a picture of a woman's insides and it explains what happens when you start to bleed. How it's not a bad thing but just means you can have babies once a month if you want and that you will need a special belt and a good supply of sanitary napkins. I had planned to just keep the book for myself, but once I told Marilyn about it, she wouldn't leave me alone. "Couldn't you just bring it outside, so we could have a good look at it? Couldn't I take it home for one night and bring it back in the morning? Couldn't I? I'll hide it in the dash of the old car. No one would have to know I had it." Finally, just so she would leave me alone, I traded her the book for a quarter and a bag of black licorice.

Mama clears her throat and says to Mrs. Morris, "You can't tell a thing about what Mona says." Her sewing machine is zipping along full speed. It's the kind with a place for your feet to move up and down to keep it going. A while ago, a stranger came by and wanted to buy it. He said they were taking the insides out of them and using them for tables in restaurants up in Toronto. The back of his truck was full of old sewing machines. He offered Mama a hundred dollars and said she could get a brand-new Singer for that and still have money left over, but in the end she said no. She said she'd be afraid to sew with anything else. Mama slows down her sewing and says, "Mona does a lot of her talking for attention."

"Oh, I know," Mrs. Morris sighs, "but I don't think she'd say she was going through the change if she wasn't. Besides, she looks flushed. She's the color of a beet most of the time."

Marilyn leans in and gives me a serious stare. "All those people up the road lie."

Marilyn has never wanted me to like Mona's girl. It seems silly that I can't have more than one friend, but if I even mention Audrey's name, Marilyn gets mad at me. I squeeze my finger to see if I can make any blood come out where I stuck it yesterday. Marilyn is tapping her cut finger against her lips the way you would a sticky sucker. It has a sliver of a scab on it. "Marilyn, we had blood come out of us yesterday. Does that mean we went through a change?"

Marilyn thinks for a minute. "That's a different kind of blood."

"What makes it different?"

She thinks for a minute. "The blood that comes out of you when you are a woman tends to be redder."

Sister and Bucky have come downstairs. Sister has been getting the babies settled for their afternoon nap. I twist around and look in the window. Bucky stands beside Mama watching her turn the wheel on the sewing machine. "Can I turn the super activator?" he says.

Mama smiles. "Just once."

Mrs. Morris is holding a little white dress close to her eyes, making a cross-stitch in the shape of a house on the collar. She makes a stitch, smoothes it with her finger, then holds the dress back to admire it. There's a glass thimble on her middle finger to keep the needle from pricking her.

Sister lets the cold water run and takes a glass down from the cupboard. She holds her finger under the water and waits, watching Mrs. Morris. "You don't have to take such care," she says. "The baby will only get it dirty the first time she wears it."

"That doesn't matter," Mrs. Morris sings.

Sister fills her glass. "If I get a job selling Tupperware, I'll be able to buy the kids some store clothes." She tips her glass and gulps the cold water.

Mrs. Morris slows up her rocking and lets the sewing rest on her lap. "Are you planning to stay away from your husband for good?"

Sister wipes the water from her lips, then she dabs her bruised eye with the drops. "If he keeps on hitting me, I will."

Mama's sewing machine slows down. "I don't know how she'll raise two children and work at the same time."

"Women do it all over the world, Mama, and a lot of them don't even have to."

"I can't imagine that," Mama says. Bucky is still standing over her, waiting to turn the wheel again. She is about to stitch around a pair of shorts for the baby boy. "I never wanted to be anything but a mother."

Sister rolls her eyes, then lets out a big sigh.

"Mama," I say in through the window screen, "is that true?"

Mama turns her face to me. "Yes it is, sweet pea. I don't know why. Even when I was little, I wanted to be a mother. I practiced changing my dolls and feeding them and when I went to the store I always admired that baby's face on the rice cereal."

"Yes, Lydia," Mrs. Morris says, "but who ever taught you to want to be anything else? That's just the way things were when we grew up. Women made mothering their life."

"That's right, Mrs. Morris," Sister says. "Things are changing now, they have to."

Marilyn pulls on my wrist for me to turn back around. It's a hazy hot day. Bucky comes out of the house and hangs over the verandah railing. The knees of his pants are worn out and one sneaker is loose and unlaced. "Do you want to play?" Marilyn asks him.

"Play what?"

"How about house?" she says, excited.

"No, I'm not playing house with you."

"Why not, Bucky?"

"House is for girls," he says and heads out to the yard. Marilyn goes after him and he hurries along. "House is not just for girls," she says.

Bucky turns around. He stops and holds his arm out straight like a sword. He slashes it back and forth in front of Marilyn and she stops still. I know Marilyn kissed Bucky once in the old car. He wanted to play inside it but she said the only way he could come in was if he kissed her. It was just a quick smack directly on her lips. I don't think it meant anything to Bucky, but Marilyn hasn't been the same since. She turns, waving Bucky away, then walks back to the verandah. "Someday, he'll want to play house with me," she says, "and I'm not gonna let him."

Marilyn gets settled back in the verandah chair just in time to see Mona and Audrey walk by. It's Wednesday so they're going to prayer meeting. They always start out early because their church is a long way away. Mona has her hair braided around her head and she's walking fast, pulling Audrey along by the hand. I can't keep from running out to the road and Bucky follows me. We walk in the ditch, alongside of them. "Hi, Audrey," I say.

Audrey smiles. Her blouse is gapping between the buttons and her tummy skin is the color of cream. Marilyn is calling my name from the verandah, but I don't look back. She keeps hollering, "You are *my* friend, remember."

Audrey watches me. I wonder why her mother doesn't make her comb her hair. It's all knotted and messy. "You and your brother wanna come with us?" she says.

"Can't," I say.

Bucky picks up a long twig and swats it back and forth at the weeds. "Mama says we can't go in your church 'cause you talk in tongues."

Mona keeps her face forward, but her eyes drop down to look at us. Audrey looks up at her. "Mama, you're squeezing my hand too tight. Let go."

Mona keeps her grip tight and Audrey starts to whine. Mona's face turns red and blotchy. "It wouldn't be that you're having your change of life," I ask.

Mona stops and turns and looks right at me. Her bottom teeth are showing. They are dark like she's been eating black licorice. It's so hot out here near the road that my face feels like I'm too close to a fire. Mona's white hanky is stuffed down her V-neck dress. The ends of it are sticking out like two thin feathers. "You kids *git* home," she says. "G'wan—*git*."

She turns and snaps Audrey's arm. Audrey twists her head back and watches us. Her eyes are round and frowning. I wave bye, but it doesn't change her look. Marilyn is hollering for Bucky now, stretching his name out long and slow. "What did you ask Mona that for?" Bucky says.

"None of your beeswax," I say.

He takes off, swatting his twig this way and that. Mad bugs fly up out of the long grass.

When we get home, Sister is on the old quilt getting ready to sun herself. She is rubbing baby oil up and down her legs. Marilyn is watching her.

"Don't stand so close, Marilyn," Sister says. "You're making a shade."

Marilyn takes two steps back and says, "Where does baby oil come from?"

Sister looks up and squints. "Well, not from babies, Marilyn. I can assure you of that." She drops the straps of her flowered bathing suit and shows her white lines to the sun. Her bubble gum snaps and pops between her teeth. Sister only chews gum when she is sitting in the sun. I sit down on the edge of the quilt. "Do you like being a mama?" I ask.

She puts her sunglasses on and stares straight ahead. "Sometimes."

Bucky comes up and Sister looks at him. "What was Mona in such a huff about? You could see her heels kicking up dust clear back here."

Bucky toes the grass, then whips the twig near my head. "Because she went and asked Mona if she was having a change of life."

"You what?"

"I didn't mean nothing by it." I stare at the magazine beside Sister. There's a blond girl with glossy lipstick on the cover. The magazine is called *True Stories*.

"You don't go around asking people that," Sister scolds, then throws her head back and laughs. "My Lord, girl, you're lucky she didn't swat you."

"Yeah," Marilyn says. "The change can make people do awful things. It can make them kill themselves and it can make them kill others."

"It cannot, Marilyn," Sister says. She pulls her magazine up to her face and flips through it. Sister told me once that her magazines were full of stories about love.

Marilyn sits down beside me. "Well," she says, "it makes them lie. I know that for a fact."

Bucky runs up on the verandah and tells Mama what I said to Mona, then disappears behind the house. Mama looks out the window for me. Her chin is in the air and her mouth gently opens. She gets up and comes out.

Mrs. Morris comes right behind her, carrying her sewing basket and fanning her face with her other hand, which still has the thimble on it. "C'mon, Marilyn, let's go home."

Marilyn presses her finger toward me. "Blood sisters," she says. Mrs. Morris reaches down and grabs her by the sister finger. She pulls her toward the road. I remember how Marilyn's blood gushed out, but mine came in slow drops.

I look at Mama.

"Why did you say that to Mona?" she asks me.

I think it might be better to be Audrey or Marilyn right now.

Sister puts her magazine down and watches Mama and me. She pulls a string from the pink gum in her mouth, then twirls it around her finger and puts it back in. Her sunglasses are exactly like a movie star's.

"Why?" Mama says again.

"I thought it was a nice thing to say."

Sister begins to giggle. Mama bites her bottom lip to hold back a smile. "The change of life is a private matter," Mama says.

"You and Mrs. Morris were talking about it."

"But that's woman talk," Mama says. "It's not for girls."

She goes back in the house and through the window I watch her lift the sewing machine and drop it back in its cabinet. If you didn't know it had a sewing machine inside, you'd think it was a plain table. One of the babies starts to cry. "Oh shoot," Sister says. "I just got out here."

She tosses her magazine and runs in the house. Her oily legs have left their shapes on the quilt. I open Sister's magazine and there is a picture of a man kissing a woman's neck. Bucky comes up. "You're not supposed to look at that," he says. "Mama says it's a dirty magazine."

I throw the magazine down and then head into the house. Mama is dusting the top of the sewing machine cabinet. I imagine her as a waitress in a restaurant in Toronto.

I slump on the couch and chew my fingernail. Mama stops dusting. "What is it?" she says. "What?"

"Everything I say is wrong."

Mama leaves the cloth on the table. She comes over and pulls me up. She hugs my head into her stomach. It's warm and gurgling. "No," she says. "Don't ever think that."

I remember the picture of a woman's insides in Sister's book. There seemed to be two of everything. The part of Mama I'm resting my head on showed a map where the change comes from. There were just a few curving lines marking it out and it wasn't hard to follow. Sister's one baby crying makes the other one start up. "Ssh, ssh," Sister hisses and then she slaps one of them.

"Stop."

Eddie

From the verandah, I see my big brother Eddie coming up the road. Sister is out by the side of the road leaning her head into her man's car. Sister's man comes around every day this time to woo her back, but you can tell by the way she crosses her legs then plants her feet solid on the dusty ground that she has not made up her mind. Whenever I go near the car to listen to them, I can smell Sister's man. His brown hair is combed back wet and he smells like he has too many splashes of Old Spice on him. Sister still has a black bruise and a little cut near her eye, where he hit her a while back. I wonder if seeing it makes him wince up inside.

I lean over the verandah railing and let my arms dangle. Eddie is getting closer all the time. I reach down at the grass that has rooted itself around the cellar of our house and grab a slivery green blade, then put it between my thumbs to blow. The sound that comes out is like the quack of a scared goose.

Mama is drying the breakfast dishes and humming herself a song about Jesus. Her humming floats through the black screen. Bucky is in the little room watching "The Friendly Giant" on television. The giant says, *Look up, look way up and I'll call Rusty.* Sister's babies are in there with him, sucking on their plastic toys. The sounds around me make me hazy and warm. They would be a nice thing to just keep on hearing and I wish that Jesus would stop time still and let me linger in them the way spiders do in their webs.

Eddie has almost got his black boots on our land when I turn and say, "Mama, Mama, guess who's here."

She looks through the screen at me with her shallow blue eyes. Between us, on the windowsill, there's a dusty flowering cactus, and its two tall arms frame Mama's face. A breeze makes the red blooms flutter. Mama lifts her eyes to find Eddie. She spots him right away on the flat yard before us. Mama walks out on the verandah, wiping her hands on the dishcloth. Her hair blows itself free from the bobby pins at the back of her head.

"Eddie," she breathes. A smile takes place on her face like a change you watch happen in the weather. She lets the screen door slam and puts the dishcloth on the railing. Mama fixes herself, smoothing her wrinkled dress down over her tummy. She drops her head and takes a couple of pins from her hair, biting them between her teeth while she pulls her hair back tight and repins it. Mama's teeth are crooked.

Eddie has been in reform school for driving drunk without a license. You can tell when he gets close to us that he has missed a lot of the good summer, because his skin is blue white under his black curly hair. It makes me sorry that he has been without the feel of the sun for so long.

Sister's man spins his dirty blue car off while Sister and Eddie walk in from the road together. There is a dust cloud bigger than all of us rising up behind them. Mama steps down to meet Eddie. He doesn't warm up to her kisses or hugging. Sister squints in the sunlight and watches them.

"You're thin," Mama says to him, but he doesn't answer her. He hangs his thumbs from his jean pockets and looks down toward the old wellhouse and the clothesline where the Monday-morning sheets are swaying in the breeze. I think how those sheets will smell when I get in bed tonight, how they will be as nice as sleeping outdoors.

After a bit, Eddie looks back to Mama and a little snarl has worked its way into his lips. "Why didn't you bail me out?"

"Oh, Eddie," Mama soothes. "You know we don't have that kind of money."

"You could have got it," he says and his voice is husky and deeper than it was before he went to jail. He walks past Mama and into the house. We watch without moving until even his shadow is gone. When we all take a breath, Eddie being home could just be something we dreamed.

Sister touches Mama's shoulder and begins one of her long talks. "Well," she says, excited, "he's got a job," the "he" being her man in the baby blue car. "He's got a job and he wants me and the babies back. He's going to work with the road crew on the new TransCanada Highway upriver and he wants to move our trailer up there into a nice park where all the other crewmen's wives live. He says he's been there and a lot of those wives have put flower boxes on their trailer windows and he says it looks as if they've been there forever.

Can you imagine that, Mama? Flower boxes on a trailer, who would have ever thought of such a thing?"

Mama's gaze looks to be caught somewhere between Sister's spray of words and the echo of Eddie's boots thumping up the stairs to his room.

"And Mama," Sister says, tapping Mama's shoulder, "he's done drinking. He's finished and won't ever touch me or the bottle again." Sister pushes her hands down to her sides and straightens up tall. "He Won't Hit Me No More," she says as firm as a mama scolding her child for sneaking candy from a store shelf.

Eddie lifts up his bedroom window and sticks his head out. We all look up at him, holding our hands over our eyes to hide them from the sun. We stand very still like he might be a king coming out to talk to his people.

"Who the hell took my room over?" He's throwing Sister's things out the window. A pair of peach pedal pushers comes down first, then her dress with the blood from her cut eye, then a white blouse and a pair of pink panties that have *Saturday* embroidered on them. The cigarette package that Eddie had rolled up in the sleeve of his T-shirt flies down from his arms swinging so much. I go over and pick it up. Mama sees me and makes her voice stern. "Don't touch those," she says, coming over and slapping me on the back. I throw them in under the bleeding heart plant beside the house.

"Don't worry, Eddie," Sister hollers. "I'm leaving and if you don't mind, I'll be doing my own packing."

Eddie slams the window down and the glass in it rattles. We watch the window until we're sure that it's not going to break, then spread out away from one another like tadpoles.

When Daddy comes home from his new job at the county garage, Bucky and I are sitting on the verandah with Sister and her babies. Her bags are all ready and the babies are in their new matching bonnets that Mama and Mrs. Morris have made. They lift their fat arms and slap their hands on their legs when they see Daddy. They sing, *DaDa DaDa DaDa.*

"I'm going back to my man," Sister hollers out. Daddy steps out of the car with his newspaper folded under his arm, as much a part of him as his black hair and loose walk. "I know what you're thinking," Sister says, "but he's gone on the wagon and when he doesn't drink, he doesn't hit me."

Daddy's dark skin is shiny from the day's heat. He

looks down at the ground and takes a white hanky from his back pocket. He wipes his forehead. "You do what's right for you and the kids," he says. I believe those words set Sister free, because a smile breaks through and she starts bouncing the babies up and down the way I would my dollies.

I walk out to touch Daddy's pant leg and Bucky copycats me. "Eddie's home," I whisper.

"Yeah," Bucky says, crossing his arms, "and he's been sleeping the whole day." All afternoon, Bucky and I have sneaked up the stairs to peek in at Eddie sleeping on top of his covers, his blue white hands sprawled out at his sides like he was dead.

"I know he's here," Daddy says. "Your mama called me and said so." He walks around the car to open the trunk. It's a big yawning mouth lifting on its own. Inside, there's a red electric guitar and an amplifier. "I got this for him."

"Whoa," Bucky says.

Daddy smiles a long smile at the shiny guitar like it might have special powers. Like it might be able to get right out of that trunk. Like it might turn Eddie into a hard-working boy.

Mama, who has been making a Sunday supper even

though it's not Sunday, comes out on the verandah and admires each of us. "It just came to me that we are all together," she says. She puts her most gentle look on Sister. "I think you should stay for supper," but she has no sooner said that than we hear the baby blue car's horn out by the road.

We squint to see Sister's man who doesn't drive into our yard or even look our way. He just sits there waiting, reminding me of one of those taxi cars you see on television.

Sister stands up and gathers her babies into her. Each of them belongs to one side of her. "Daddy," she says, smiling, "can you take my bags out for me?"

"Wouldn't he come in and have supper with us?" Mama asks. "You never know when we'll all be together again."

"Oh, no," Sister sighs. "He's too embarrassed for hitting me. In time, Mama," she smiles, her dark eye still lost in its bruise, "he'll come round."

Mama rubs her hands up and down Sister's bare arms. "You don't have to go if you don't want to. We can make room."

"I know," Sister says.

"And you don't have to stay with him if things get

bad," Mama adds, kissing Sister on her dropped head. Mama admires the babies' faces and touches them lightly with her fingertips. "Babies are a comfort, aren't they?"

Sister nods yes, moving away from Mama. "I'll write to you," she smiles.

Bucky and I follow Sister out to the road. Daddy puts their belongings down for Sister's man to get out and take. He gets out quick, but he doesn't let his eyes look at anyone, not even his own babies.

"You be good to her and the kids," Daddy says.

The man stops in his tracks with his back to us and his neck veins go red. "I've got work up north," he says.

"You think that will make the difference, do you?"

"Yes sir," Sister's man says. He gets in the car and looks straight ahead, over the big steering wheel.

Sister steps up on her toes to kiss Daddy's face. "Don't worry," her voice goes with the coo of one of those birds that hide in the trees and cry in the early morning.

Daddy hugs his arms around Sister and the babies. His lips are held tight like he has captured something inside of him that he doesn't want to let go. I brush up to them. Sister makes room for me to squeeze in and hug her waist. She smells of lilacs. She should do like Mama says and be careful of her man. I imagine her as a cooing bird flying straight into a window she doesn't even know is there.

Mama waves bye from the verandah. We all watch Sister and her babies drive off to their new life. Sister's man has a white pretend cat in his back window. Its head wobbles up and down. I figure it's trying to tell us something. *Uh-huh, uh-huh, uh-huh,* it says. I hang on to Daddy's hand. Bucky picks up a stone and throws it at the back of the moving car.

Eddie doesn't come down for supper so we eat our roast chicken and stuffing real quiet. It's hard not to stare at his clean shiny plate. The table is big and empty without Sister and her babies. I wonder how far away from us they have traveled and if everything is still okay.

"Oh, I wish he'd come down," Mama says, looking up at the ceiling. "He probably hasn't had one decent thing to eat since he was—" The word "arrested" sticks in her throat and doesn't come up. "He's so thin and pale looking."

Mama's lips float open and shudder. Daddy reaches out and puts his tanned hand over her white one. "It's all right, Lydia," he says. For a while, those words help us get our supper down.

Daddy has already given Eddie his guitar. He starts to play it above us. He plays as good as someone who has always known how.

"Oh," Mama says, pulling her hand back from Daddy's. She pulls it back so fast that I wonder if Daddy's hand burnt it. "I wish you hadn't bought that thing for him. It's not going to make a bit of difference."

"You don't know that," Daddy says. "I'm sure no one knows what would make a difference with him."

Mama stands up and starts to clear the table. "It won't be something as worldly as an electric guitar, I can guarantee you that. Besides, it's always been a set of drums that he wanted."

"They didn't have any drums," Daddy says.

"Well, you shouldn't have bothered getting anything."

Daddy bangs his hand down flat on the table. "What do you want me to do, then?"

Their stare is firm. I imagine an invisible wire running between them, holding their heads stiff.

"I want you to use a little authority and not be coming home here with expensive gifts for him when he's been in reform school for three months." Mama talks fast and her voice shakes.

Daddy clears his throat. "But you made a special supper for him and that's all right."

Mama's face floods red. "He needs to eat. He needs the basics."

Bucky watches Mama and Daddy real close. He leans in over his plate toward them. His eyes float back and forth watching the words they fire at each other. I want to get out quick so their fighting won't get in me.

In the yard, I see Marilyn standing out on her lawn with her hands on her hips, looking over at our house. "What's that noise?" she hollers.

"Eddie," I say. "Playing his new *gee*-tar." She shakes her head the way an old person would and walks back into her house. I suppose her mama and daddy have been wondering the same thing. She's going to be the first one to tell them. *You'll never guess what that jailbird is doing now,* she'll say.

I take my kazoo out of my pocket. It used to be Daddy's, but he gave it to me. I lie down on the grass to play it. When I blow my kazoo, the sound of Mama and Daddy arguing disappears. I play it for Jesus, who I know is up there watching me. I play it just as pretty as I can because if He wanted to, He could make things better here. I keep time with Eddie's guitar sounds and I think how if we were like families on television, we would all be sitting around the supper table. We would eat piled-up Jell-O cubes with whipped cream and tell one another how good our day was.

Bucky sticks his head out of Eddie's window to yell at me. "Guess what he's playing?"

When I sit up my back is damp from the early night coming up from the ground. "What?" I ask.

"'Wipe Out,'" Bucky yells down, shaking his fists in the air and smiling.

"That's not very Christian," I say, because I'm lost for words and because I think that's what Mama would say to Eddie if she could make herself, if she could just stop being afraid that he would leave and never come back. Eddie turns up the volume and the twanging twists and turns through our yard. It reminds me of the buzz of the Tasmanian Devil. I plug my ears and try to squeeze the sound out of my head.

A big old car rumbles into our driveway. Since I'm the only one out here, I do what Daddy likes us to do and walk over to it. There's a red-skinned teenager with a burning cigarette hanging in his lips. I just stand there and chew at my fingernail, watching him until he notices me. "Eddie home?" he asks.

"Yep," I say. "He just got back from jail and Daddy bought him a brand-new *gee*-tar."

"What for?" he asks.

I don't know what for really, so I just stand there and swing my hips round, like Mama does with the babies, while I tap my kazoo on my front bottom teeth.

Eddie rips out of the house with Daddy right behind him. "You stay home, Eddie. There's no need in getting in with the same crowd that got you in jail."

"Nobody got me in jail," Eddie smirks. He bangs a hello on the hood of his friend's car and goes around to climb in.

Daddy comes after him, grabs his T-shirt, then pulls him back by the neck. They scratch at each other and their feet twist underneath them in a struggle. I stand still. They're making the dust rise.

"I'll do what I damn well want," Eddie says, his teeth gritted. He brings his fist up quick and catches Daddy under his chin. Daddy gets a stung look on his face. Blood comes out of his mouth. This is the second time in not that long that blood has dripped down onto our ground. First Sister, now Daddy. I've noticed that blood makes a black stain when it soaks into the dirt and I wonder how long it takes for bloodstains to go away. Daddy's blood has made him madder. He gets Eddie in a headlock and bangs the side of his face on the hood of the rusty car. It makes a loud popping noise. Mama and Bucky are in the doorway, watching. Mama hollers out for Daddy not to hurt Eddie.

I think of the dream I had of Mama last night. She was showing me the picture album and she was saying, *Here you are when you were one year old and here you are with Bucky when I made you that picnic in the yard and you both had strawberry jam all over your faces. Oh yes, and remember this? This is when you got into the poison ivy and your face swelled all up. Oh, you were a sight. And here you are with a new Easter hat.* That dream was telling me, This is your place, this is where you belong. Just like Mama and Daddy are trying to tell Eddie right now.

Daddy holds Eddie's neck tight with the twisted white T-shirt and my brother's face is growing redder by the minute.

Mama bursts out the door. "Let go of him," she yells. "You'll kill him."

Bucky comes out right behind her and he starts to cry because Eddie is his idol.

Daddy pushes him against the old car. "Go then," he says. "Suit yourself."

Eddie catches his breath and climbs into the car, shrugging off Daddy's last touch. He tries to smile like nothing has happened. We all take in a wobbly breath and the two boys are gone before we even realize they're leaving. The yard is quiet. I suppose that it's tired of everything that has gone on here. Mama steps out on the verandah. "I shouldn't have told you to be hard on him. What if he doesn't come back? What if he gets into trouble again? What if he's in an accident?"

Daddy wipes the blood from his mouth and just stares at Mama. "If he comes home drunk, he won't be spending any more time under this roof." His words move fast like flung stones with sharp edges.

Mama points her finger at Daddy. "Do you see what alcohol has done to this family? Do you?"

Daddy looks away from her, then walks down toward the wellhouse, where his beer is always waiting cool in case things go wrong. He walks just like the man on prison grounds that I saw on TV. We watch him until he goes inside and closes the door.

Mama turns from the big yard and goes into the

kitchen. Bucky follows her. I hear the tap water start up. Mama will wash the dishes, then dry them hard like the trim around the edges is a stain itself.

The television comes on and through the window I can see Bucky. His head is as round as an orange. He's sitting in front of the moving pictures and soon he'll be hypnotized.

I stay out in the new night to blow on my kazoo. The sounds that come out are short and weak. I blow it anyway. I figure Jesus could be listening.

Three Hearts

The morning after the big snowstorm Mama is sick. Her hair has twisted itself into knots like spikes all over her head and she is so weak that her words are puffy and low. We are all up, listening to the radio that sits on top of the fridge to see if there will be any school. Bucky and I sit at the wooden table that wobbles and wait with our elbows pressed into the plastic tablecloth. Mama is lying on the kitchen couch, wrapped in her red robe, rolling her head from side to side, sighing.

Her eyes are the color of faded jeans and when she talks she sounds scared, so I go over and stand by her head. I take one of Daddy's newspapers from under the couch and fan her. The newspaper leaves black on my finger so I rub it onto my corduroys. Mama has *nerves,* and when my brother Eddie drinks, they get worse. She says that nothing could make her more weak than the fact that she has a fifteen-year-old child with a drinking problem.

Daddy says Eddie has an angry streak like steel running through his heart. He quit school last year and now he sleeps all morning and stays out all night. He drinks with a boy called Cake who lives on welfare and drives a big car. Mama and Daddy can't manage Eddie. They tried to make him go back to school, but whenever they brought it up his temper would roll and he would slam himself at the walls. I remember Mama telling Daddy that maybe Eddie shouldn't go to school, that maybe his whole problem was that the teacher picked on him. But Daddy told her right up quick that Eddie had drinking in his blood just like Daddy's whole family did. Daddy used to drink every weekend. He'd go to the legion on Friday night after supper and sometimes not come home until Saturday morning. The last time I saw my daddy real drunk, his lip was broken wide open and purple. "Who did that to you?" Mama said.

"My brother." Daddy made the words sound as if they were the last ones left in him. They reminded me of the bobcat we heard once, caught in the wire fence way down in the field, snarling.

Mama wrinkled her forehead. "Why? Why did he hit you?"

One of Daddy's eyes went wet. "Because he was drunk, too."

Mama blames herself for everything. When I smile at Mama, she always says, "Poor girl, she's got her mama's crooked teeth," but I always say, "Mama, I grew these teeth, not you."

"I'm so warm," Mama says, and I think of calling Daddy at the county garage to see what to do with her, but I figure he's sure to be out plowing the roads with all this snow. Mama is sicker than usual because Eddie didn't come home and she sat up all night waiting for him. In the night I could hear the rocking chair in Eddie's room moving back and forth like a song. I knew Mama had her face wrapped in her cool hands. I stroke her hair and she says to the air, "You wonder if he's dead or alive."

The radio is playing "O happy day / When Jesus washed / My sins away." How do they get all those singers in the radio station so early in the morning, I wonder. Bucky is still waiting at the table. "I wish they'd say school's canceled," he says.

"It is," I guess, and stand on the chair and press my

forehead against the top part of the window so I can see out over the snow. In the shiny glass I can see my ghost looking back at me so I blow steam on the window and make three little hearts that Mama will complain about later. Big cutout flakes are still coming down. The verandah is a lake of snow, swirling up and around the railing and window in waves. I think of my feet sinking deep into the new snow, then I think of Eddie frozen in a snowbank.

"Upper Valley Elementary," Bucky yells. "We're closed. No school." He jumps up from the table and does a little circle. "Mama, where are my snow pants? Mama?"

He rubs Mama's face the way you polish an apple and a smile sneaks out from under her half-moon lips.

When Eddie comes home, Bucky and I are in the hallway putting bread bags over our wool socks so our feet won't get wet. All dressed in black, he's walking like a puppet. A cigarette is burning at the side of his mouth and he steps over us like we are stones.

"Eddie." Mama sits up. "Where have you been? I'm sick from waiting. What do you do all night?"

Eddie doesn't answer Mama. He gives her one of those stares that Daddy says could freeze hell and Mama stands up in front of him.

"Eddie," she begs. He uses his long blue hand to push her back down on the couch. The jolt chokes her. She cries like a baby that got its feelings hurt. Before he goes upstairs, Eddie tosses his cigarette in the sink. He smells drunk. I twist a hole through the bread bag, listening for Mama to stop being sad. Bucky is all ready to go.

Mama wipes her face, pulling herself up. She ties her robe as tight as a package, then takes her pills from her pocket. "I need some sleep," she says to the bottle.

She comes into the hallway and steps over the water spots that Eddie left. Her feet are so pink. "Will you be warm enough?" She ties a green scarf around my neck and looks down at my face. "I want you to stop painting your lips," she says. I do it with Mercurochrome. Mama rubs my lips with her thumbs until they burn.

She holds my face in her hands and looks to Bucky. "Double up on your mittens, Bucky. You don't want to freeze to death."

Mama leans on the door frame and watches us march out the door. "Have fun," she says. "Your mama's going to lie down."

The snow is white and heavy like flour. Bucky pushes the wooden storm door closed behind us and we fall on our knees, piling the snow up at the door like we want to bury it.

"Now Mama can rest," Bucky says and he packs the cracks with lots of snow.

I love Bucky's face. It comes out at you and always looks to smile like a dolphin's, and even though he's thirteen months younger than me, he seems older. He has his hands on his hips like a man. We wade out to the yard and the snow is so deep and heavy that we just stop for a long time and look at things. My breathing is even with his. The white cover is perfect except for Eddie's footprints coming in from the road. I look at them and I'm so happy that he came home, it makes me want to get right down and kiss where he's walked. Across the road, the snow swirls around Marilyn Morris's house. The tiny wind smells brand new and the telephone wires have so much snow on them they are almost invisible. The snowflakes try to get in our eyes. We have to squint to see each other.

"Catch them on your tongue," Bucky says. We tilt our heads back and stretch our tongues to our chins. Bucky's tongue is the color of watermelon.

We pull our scarves up over our noses. My breath is warm and wet on the wool. I look back at the house and in the fuzzy snow it's a big blank face. The windows are as dark as molasses. Nothing moves in them. I think of Eddie hidden in a stack of pillows with his mouth open, while the wind whispers around his window. I think how Daddy will pull him out of bed when he comes home. "I told you to look for work today," he'll say and Eddie will squirm out of Daddy's hands the way he always does.

"Let's make angels," Bucky says.

The yard is as smooth as white marble. We drop down on our backs and slide our arms like we're trying to fly. We make so many angels that there is no untouched snow left. I tell Bucky if the birds were out, they'd think it was an angel graveyard. We wade around the house to look at all the high drifts. There is a huge drift in front of the shed that is connected to our house, so we go around where there is a wooden ladder and climb up on the shed's roof. The roof is slippery, but we know if we fall we'll just land in the soft snow and laugh. We slide down the roof into the drift and the snow comes up to our hips. Bucky pretends he's in quicksand. He waves his arms and screams, "Help, I'm drownin', help me."

"Kick your knees," I say half-mad, and he pushes himself free, giggling.

We're lined up on the roof like pigeons when we hear the snowplow coming. We push off together, landing just in time to see Daddy go by. He honks and we rush out of the snow so we can run and see him. The legs of our snow pants hiss. When we get there, there's nothing but a swirl of white dust and the low growl of Daddy's machine going over the far side of the dirt road. After that, everything is soft and still.

We scuff our boots through the snow to erase the angels. We make foot holes in a big bank of snow by the road and climb up to the top. The snow is all packed hard. The top of the bank is as flat as a stage. As soon as I get up there, Bucky pushes me off. That's what Eddie used to do when he played with us, that's exactly what he did and Bucky has learned it from him. I slide down over the bank and land on my back.

"I'm the king of the castle and you're the dirty rascal," he sings. I don't move. I let the snow whip around my face and I stay perfectly still until the ends of my fingers go numb.

"Sis," Bucky says, "Sissy, get up. C'mon, let's play. Come back up."

He climbs down beside me. "You're not dead," he says and kicks a pile of snow in my face.

Then he starts digging a tunnel in the side of the bank. We dig and round it out like an igloo. It's warmer on the inside. When we're finished, Bucky leans back against the hard wall and sucks the snow from his mitten.

"Bucky, don't eat snow, it's got worms in it."

"It does not." He wipes his nose with the back of his jacket sleeve.

"Mama says it does."

"It's not snow, it's blubber," he says and just the thought of it makes me laugh.

"Get some icicles," he says.

The icicles are always my job. Bucky says Eskimo women do all the stuff like that. "Anything they can do without their husbands' help, they do. They're brave," he told me once.

I climb up on the verandah railing and grab one big icicle to knock the rest down. The icicles tick off as I move across the railing. They fall like darts in the snow. I dig them out and carry them back for kindling. We use the tips of the icicles to draw on the walls of the igloo. I always draw a trailer because I'd like to live in one when I grow up, just like Sister. I try to draw flower boxes on the trailer's windows, but it isn't easy. Today, Bucky tries to draw Eddie with a huge set of drums. Eddie likes the Beatles. He combs his black hair down over his forehead and seals it with Dippity-Do so he looks like Ringo. Sometimes when Bucky and I come home from school, Eddie is sitting in Daddy's brown recliner beating the arms of the chair with two wooden spoons. His timing is even and his blue eyes are storm clouds when he plays. "Get away from me," he always says. I don't think he knows that we just like what he's doing and want to watch him.

We pile the icicles in the middle for firewood, because we're tired, then we lie on our backs and study the white walls. We never make any rules, but both Bucky and I know that whenever we build a house, he's the husband and I'm the wife. After a while, he leans over and kisses my cheek with his wet lips and then lies back down. We both close our eyes.

When our pretend night is over, Bucky sits up, rubbing himself all over because he's cold. "Get up," he says. "We need more firewood."

I poke my head out of the tunnel. The air is thick and

much colder. The flakes have turned into small white dots. I run through the snow to the verandah and climb up to get the icicles. In the distance, I can hear Daddy's plow. I turn and brace my feet, holding two big sticks of ice in my hands like swords. I wave the swords crossways when I see Daddy coming. I remind myself of the people on "Gilligan's Island" waving to airplanes. Snow flies up from the road and Daddy gives a big toot as he goes by and the plow looks empty, like it's driving itself. It makes me feel good that my Daddy is in there, tooting at me, even if I can't see him.

I load myself down with the firewood to carry back to the tunnel. When I can't find the igloo's hole, I start to feel dizzy. I carry the icicles back and forth all along the bank, but the whiteness is all I can see. I dump the ice and start to crawl through the heavy snow on my knees, and I say, "Bucky, Bucky."

I look back along the bank for a piece of Bucky and I dig at a dark spot hoping it's his mitten, but it's just dirt or a shadow. I stop and listen for him while the weather squeezes in around me. I'm on the verandah and I don't remember running here. The door is piled high with snow. I pull at the handle but the door won't move. I brush the snow back from it with both hands. I get it open just a tiny crack, but I still can't get inside. I jerk the handle back and forth and bang the door hard. "Eddie, Eddie," I holler after each bang.

Then the ghost in me takes over and I begin to dream. I'm dreaming while my body bangs on the door. I dream that I'm all grown up with breasts like Mama and I'm standing in front of the house screaming for Eddie to wake up. His window is black and empty. I'm screaming, "Eddie, help me. Bucky is suffocating. Eddie, help."

I dream that I climb up the side of the house toward Eddie's window. Splinters peel off the house and stick to my fingers until the tips turn purple and begin to bleed. The blood makes the wooden siding slippery and I start to slide back down to the ground. I leave long thin red scratches on the house.

I'm staring down, rubbing my frozen fingers together like I've just discovered them when Mama opens the door. Her face is foggy and I tell her fast what has happened.

"Go," she yells, pushing me out into the yard. "Show me."

I point at the flat side of the bank where I think the hole is and I'm scared that I'm wrong and that Jesus won't wash my sins away. Mama's red robe works its way open in the front and her flowered nightie looks strange out here in the snow. I watch the soles of her feet staring up with all their cracks and dryness and something about the way they twist and cuddle makes them look like two baby pigs. I wonder if they feel cold or if Mama has forgotten everything but Bucky. She's breathing with the wind.

"What happened?" She turns her face to me for the shortest second. I don't know what to say. I remember how the plow shook the windowpanes in our house when it rumbled by.

"What happened?" she says again.

"The plow," I say, "the plow came by," and then I wished I'd blamed myself. That's what Mama would have done.

She has both arms in the snow and she's talking to herself like she's praying, like the bank is her altar. I look back at the house. Why hasn't Eddie heard us? Why hasn't he come to help? I'm almost ready to let my tears out when Mama reaches way in with her head and all.

"Oh my land," she says, her words just a whisper.

She pushes her shoulders in and she gets a hold of something and pulls two or three times. I can tell she's getting tired and I'm afraid that she'll give up. She reaches one more time and hauls Bucky out by the arm. His body is limp. One double mitten slips off in the snow. He's flat on his back. Mama stares at his face, which looks tired and sleepy, and she shakes him.

"Bucky, Bucky, Bucky," she's says quick like his name is a rhyme. She puts her ear on his mouth and listens. She opens her thin lips and puts them on his in a circle. Specks of snow float down and land on her hair. Bucky opens one eye and squints at the flakes.

"Bucky," Mama says soft and pushes her face against his cheeks, first one side, then the other. She holds his head on both sides. Bucky reaches his hand up to Mama as she pulls him to her chest. He snuggles into her flowered nightie. Mama's lips are shaking and her eyes are watery blue like a well that you look down into.

"It's all my fault," she says. "I shouldn't have been sleeping in the day." She lifts Bucky up on his feet, keeping her hands under his arms. His face is red and full and I touch his bare fingers, which hang down in the wind like leaves.

"Come, baby," Mama says.

Bucky walks on his own, but Mama holds him tight.

Her red robe flies in the wind behind them and the way it swirls and prances around her makes her look as if she's dancing.

I fall back and let my bottom make itself a snug chair in the snow. I'm jerky on the inside and my stomach is small and hard. I thought Bucky would be dead and that his face would be caved in from the heavy snow. I pick up his mitten and try to forget the melted look I thought he would have when Mama pulled him out. I take the mitten apart. The inside one is blue. The outside one is an old gray mitten of Eddie's, full of holes. I push through the holes wondering how they got there. Each hole has a string of wool in it so I pull on the yarn to make the hole bigger, but the hole puckers together in a kiss. I fix every hole this way until the mitten rumples itself into a little ball.

I look at our house. Orange light comes from the kitchen and shadows move past the window in slow motion. I bet Mama is rubbing Bucky's chest with Vicks VapoRub. I think of his round chest that juts out in the middle and my throat goes full and tight. I listen and everything is big and quiet. I wonder if Daddy will come home soon. I stuff Eddie's gray mitten inside of Bucky's and waddle myself free from the snow.

Baptism

Mama is taking Eddie to get his crooked teeth fixed. She lifts the china teapot down from the cupboard and picks off its cover like a berry, then pulls out the saved money bills. There are twos and fives and tens, more money than I've ever seen. She smoothes each bill out on the counter.

Eddie still comes home drunk every night even though Daddy said a long while back that he would kick him right out of the house if he kept on doing it. I think Daddy pretends not to hear him when he stumbles in late. Once, somebody that Eddie had been out with just stopped his car out by the road and pushed Eddie from it. I didn't see, but I heard Mama crying and telling Daddy. She said he looked as helpless as a sack of kittens when he rolled into the ditch by our yard. The moon was out that night and the beams made a silver wand on my bedroom floor. "Let him stay right out there," I heard Daddy say. "Just stop trying to drag him in."

Mama had been out in her nightgown begging Eddie to get up, and when he didn't, she hauled him all the way across the lawn to the gravel driveway. She told Daddy that she didn't want to drag him any farther because the gravel would scratch his face. While they talked, I waved at the wand the moonbeam had made.

"Where'd you get all that money, Mama?" I ask.

"I saved up Eddie's family allowance checks. Ever since he was born, when I got that twelve dollars each month from the government, I cashed it and put the money in my good teapot."

"Why'd Eddie get money from the *government*?"

"Oh, you all do," Mama says. "Every child in Canada does."

I think about that and then I say, "Have you got a teapot for me?"

Mama reaches down and touches my face. "I've used yours for things you needed," she says.

"Like what?" I ask.

"Oh, clothes and shoes and school supplies, and a few times, when your daddy has been out of work, I've even used it to buy groceries."

I touch a crisp two-dollar bill. Its pinkness reminds me of the inside of a salmon. I think about Eddie's teapot of money the way I would a nest of robin's eggs. When I find eggs that have been tucked away close to me somewhere and I never even knew, it comes as a nice surprise.

"Did you know Eddie's teeth were going to be crooked when he was born?" I ask.

"Oh, no," Mama says. "I saved the money thinking that it might help him get a good education." She says this soft. I can almost see the dream come out of her mouth and float around with the dust specks in the sunlight.

"Will braces make him stop drinking?"

Mama stops and listens, her eyes searching out the window. I listen too, but there's only the hot humming of bugs in the earth.

"Well," she begins, then stops and pulls in a long breath. She blinks her eyes the way a genie does, trying to make the question go away. After a bit, I think she knows that the question will stay between us until it hears her voice. "He has already had the impressions done," she says, "but today is when he actually gets the braces on. Of course, it's late," she says, smoothing the money with her white fingers. "He's sixteen now and that's late for braces."

The stumble of Mama's words makes more questions inside of me. I look up at her and her heart blood has come up and filled her beauty bar skin with crimson. To see it makes my own heart blood come up and it tells me to think of a better question. One that will maybe make us pretend that everything in our family is okay.

"Are the braces going to hurt him?" I ask.

"Oh, yes, for a while they will. The dentist told me that Eddie had natural crooked teeth and to make them straight is really making them unnatural. Of course, it will be better for chewing and his bite and everything." Mama lifts her head, breathing the breeze from the back window, then blows out a sigh. "You know, when his teeth are straight, he is going to be even more handsome than he already is."

Daddy comes home early from work to keep Bucky and me and so Mama can have the car to drive Eddie to the dentist. While they're getting in the car, Daddy tells Mama to drive careful, because they are working on the road. He leans on the car door, looking in at Mama. "There's a lot of machinery to look out for."

"We'll be careful," Mama says, starting the car and smiling out at Daddy. "Bye."

Bucky and I wave them off from the verandah. We watch them until they're out of sight. Mama sits up straight, her hands tight on the steering wheel. Eddie is slumped over in the passenger seat, his head resting on the door and his black curls blowing like a swarm of bats around his head. He is getting braces because Mama and Daddy say if he does he can take his driver's test after. They make deals with Eddie.

Daddy wanders out to the side of the road and so does our neighbor, Mr. Morris. They stand talking back and forth over the fresh oiled dirt like it's a river between them. The smell that it makes baking in the sun reminds me of all my summers before. Bucky and I listen to Daddy and Mr. Morris for a while, but their talk is things that we have heard before: The rain we've had. The new road crew being all Frenchmen from up north. The price of pulp going up.

Bucky and I walk down in the field behind our house, which is one year hay and one year clover. We play in the field all the time. It has been a war country crawling with enemies. It has been a huge stadium with Billy Graham preaching and me as a reformed sinner, singing "How Great Thou Art." It has been a hospital where Bucky and I worked all day to save lives. And more than once it has been a school for children who need constant punishment. We tortured one boy until he died and we had to bury him in the cemetery where most of the soldiers from the war are.

Because of the rain, the field has made a little pond. It does this every year. A long time ago Eddie had a homemade raft that he pushed around in it. He used a big stick. Mama would admire him from the verandah, her hair swaying like dark ferns around her face. He's my Huck Finn, she'd say. Bucky and I would look at her and wonder who in the world she was talking about.

We stand at the edge and the water seeps up around our sneakers, our little boats that will not take float. It's shallow near the edge. If I waded out to the center, it would only be knee-deep. White puffy clouds pass over low and fast. Bucky looks at me. His bow-tie lips are the same color that the clover will be when it comes up. Sometimes at night when Bucky kisses me, I imagine his lips leaving a stain behind. In the night, when I wake and hear Eddie stumbling in, I touch the place where Bucky's stain would be.

I reach down to test the water. Its temperature is cool. "We could have a baptism," I say.

Bucky's green eyes catch the sun. "You mean dunk each other all the way like the preacher does?"

"It's kind of cold for that," I say, "but maybe we could just sprinkle each other the way they do the newborns."

A warm wind comes up and my dress flaps against my legs. I try my best to hold it down thinking too much wind might make me take flight. Bucky leans over and cups the cold water in his hands. He lifts it up to his bow lips like he's going to drink, then he looks at me and our eyes are held together by their matching color. "Do you love the Lord Jesus as your personal Savior," he says like the preacher does before he lets people go all the way under.

"You know I do," I say.

"Then close your eyes," Bucky says.

I close them tight. Bright lights swirl in the black behind my lids. A big splash of cold water lands on my head and trickles down my face. "Ha, ha," Bucky laughs.

"Bucky," I yell, but he's off, giggling and zigzagging down through the field.

I wipe my face with my arms and turn to see Daddy up by the road, talking. He has one hand in his pocket. The other one is scratching at the side of his face. Just to see him do it makes me hear his whiskers snap under his fingernails.

Bucky starts into the woods where we are not supposed to go. I run hard, afraid that I'll lose him in all the trees and bushes. "Wait up, Bucky," I yell and he turns to me. The hair at the front of his head blows in the breeze. He does the monkey smile at me, then keeps on going.

I stop at the line between open sky and green leaves. A ball of quiet comes around me and I can hear my breath way down inside being born. The ground makes tiny snaps and noises. "Bucky," I say, "where are you? Come out, Bucky."

There is a camp deeper in the woods that Eddie and his friends built a long time ago, so that they would have a place to go and smoke. I know that's where Bucky has gone even though it's against the rules. "Stay out of that old camp," Mama always says.

I think she's afraid that sin itself is living there. She thinks this because that old camp is where Eddie started to smoke. But I've heard our preacher say that sin is a weed that grows inside of people. I always try to remember that. He says the kind of sin that's inside of most people can come up and choke them like a nasty old tapeworm.

I find Bucky sitting the way Daddy does with his knees up and his arms resting on top of them. "You can't come down here, Bucky."

"Can too," he says.

The camp is empty except for some old leaves that the wind blew in, a deck of cards wrapped in plastic, and a rusty coffee can in the corner, full of butts. I walk around the inside. "We could play school here," I say.

Before Bucky says yes or no, Daddy hollers for us. His voice is far off, but as loud as traveling thunder can be. I duck down on the camp floor and turn my face to the musty-smelling wall. Bucky gets down beside me. Daddy's voice keeps hollering out, but we don't answer because we know that we're already in trouble, and it's too late for us to do anything about it. The wind makes shivers on my legs. Daddy's voice comes again so close that Bucky giggles. We don't try to hide, just wait for Daddy to see us, so we can surrender.

I hear his shoes on the plank outside and I use my hands to make blinders for my eyes. I tighten up inside. "Why didn't you answer me?" Daddy says.

We push our backs to the wall. I want to say that I didn't hear him, but when Daddy is looking right at me, I can't lie.

"You shouldn't be down in these here woods."

"We got lost," Bucky says.

"C'mon," Daddy says. We get up and follow him with our hands behind us. He doesn't go toward home, but heads farther into the woods. He clears his throat. "I got lost in the woods once, myself."

"You did?" Bucky says, scurrying to keep up.

Daddy tells us that he and another man were cruising a piece of land and neither of them had a compass. He says they crossed a stream going in and did the same thing coming out. Daddy keeps walking strong in front of us. "But what we didn't realize," he says, "is that stream had a couple of branches to it and we were nowhere near where we went in."

The warm breeze blows and it takes my breath away easy like I'm a baby sleeping in the wind. Daddy's pant legs flap. "What did you do, Daddy?" I ask.

"When we realized we were lost, my friend just about went crazy. He took off running, first one way, then the other. I went after him, but before I could get a hold on him, he had run through a whole patch of thistle bushes and cut himself all to pieces. Even his eyes were pricked open and bleeding. When I saw them, I thought to myself, If he gets infection in his eyes, he'll go blind."

"Why did he run like that?" Bucky asks.

"Well," Daddy breathes. "He was lost and panicked. People do that. He just took to running. He was probably thinking if he ran fast enough, he would come to a clearing sooner or later."

"Did he?" Bucky asks, panting.

"No," Daddy says and stops. "He didn't and he wouldn't have. After a while, I got a hold of him and I said, 'You may as well just calm down, because I don't believe we're going anywhere tonight.'"

Bucky wipes away a mosquito perched on his lip. "Were you scared, Daddy?"

"Yes," he admits, "I was, but there wasn't any use in both of us running wild."

"What did you do then?"

"Oh, I built a little fire and we slept there and when morning came, we got our bearings and walked out. I'd heard of men doing it, but you couldn't have convinced me the night before that I'd be able to."

We watch Daddy close. "Of course, things don't always

turn out that way," he says. "Sometimes lost people just stay lost."

Daddy moves ahead of us and we scurry behind him. The mossy floor of the forest grows greener. Daddy talks to us just like Jesus would, teaching us the leaves of trees. He picks them off and lets them fall back toward us in the breeze. Some fly too high for us to catch. The white birch is my favorite tree because Daddy says the Indians used the bark to make canoes. He lets us lift a piece off to see that it's white and thin, but still strong. The inside is the color of a new penny. Its clean smell, which I love, comes off in my fingers. I'll hold my fingers to my nose in bed tonight and be reminded of the woods.

After a lot of walking, Daddy asks both Bucky and me which way it is to home. We twist around to look at the trees and then the sky. I point back through a grove of pines. Bucky says it's the other way where the light is shining through. Daddy steadies his eyes on us and says we're both wrong.

"No way," Bucky says.

Daddy points his hand like a Mountie directing traffic away from an accident. "We're going to go out between that poplar and the fir."

When Bucky and I look down at the ground, Daddy touches our heads. "You have to know an awful lot about this place not to end up lost."

At home, Eddie is out in the yard polishing the sides of Daddy's Pontiac with an old T-shirt. Underneath all the dust, the car is the green of new grass. Eddie's legs have a horseshoe shape, bowing out. The ends of his jeans are raveling and white.

"Get your license?" Daddy hollers.

Eddie turns and his lips are held tight over his teeth. He's careful not to show us his new braces when he talks. "Yep."

"That's good," Daddy says, swatting Eddie's polishing arm, which looks to have wires underneath the skin.

Eddie nods his head at Daddy and then before anything changes, he says, lisping, "Do you think I could have the car after supper?"

The sun is still bright and it makes everything shine. "I imagine," Daddy says. "No speeding or drinking, though."

Eddie chews his upper lip. "You don't need to tell me that."

Mama comes out on the verandah. She is pale like

maybe she sat in the dentist chair. Her smile is there, though, making up for the paleness. "Where've you been?"

I'm afraid that Daddy is going to tell her that Bucky and I were in the camp, but he doesn't. "Just down in the field," he says, which isn't really a lie.

Mama holds up her new Instamatic camera that Daddy gave her for Christmas. She studies us for a minute. "I want a picture of you all," she says. This reminds me of what she always tells me. She says that when you grow up your memories are just snapshots. She says they don't move, but flash on and off in your head like a siren light. Bucky and I get in front of the car and pose ourselves.

"C'mon Eddie," Mama coos.

"I don't want to," Eddie says.

"C'mon, Eddie," Mama says. "It's not every day a boy gets braces and his license all in the same afternoon."

"I'm not smilin'," he says, firm. "I don't want no one seeing these steel traps."

Daddy stands behind Bucky. Eddie reaches through the car window and pulls something out. We watch him and he holds an exact copy of his teeth in his hands. They are white and chalky. He makes the teeth do alligator snaps and we laugh at the way they look.

"I didn't know the dentist gave you your impressions," Mama says.

Eddie stands beside me and holds the impressions up beside his face in his cupped hands. His face is stiff, but the impressions look to be smiling. I guess it's a before and after.

We look to Mama and she clicks. "There," she says, "that wasn't so bad, was it?"

She smoothes her hand over her hair, then turns to go back into the smell of supper. "I'm making something soft so you'll be able to eat, Eddie." Daddy follows her. The smell is fried hamburg and boiled potatoes.

I look up at the blue skin under Eddie's chin. I bet if I held a buttercup there, it would reflect real good. The sun is on his face. His mouth is open just a silver crack. "I see your braces," I say and run away from him.

I run down toward the pond. He comes after me and so does Bucky, laughing and making hyena giggles. I stop out of breath near the pond and put my hands up. Eddie lets on that he's going to hit me, then slaps me on the head easy instead. "Say you didn't see them."

I squint and shake my head no.

Bucky catches up and points his finger at me. "She

wants to be baptized." He makes the word "she" sound like I'm a stranger to them.

"*She* does?" Eddie grabs my shoulders and rocks me back and forth. "Say you didn't see the braces," he warns.

I push my shoulders up and try to hide my head. He lifts me up in his arms. My face is close to his. He doesn't look at me before he tosses me to the water. I fly for a second, then drop straight down and land on my bottom in the soft reeds. My head goes under before I'm able to get my legs under me. I gulp down the cold water, then stand up fast and run to the edge, choking. Eddie takes off and Bucky follows him. I want to run to tell Daddy what Eddie has done, but I don't want to get things stirred up. There would be a big fuss if Daddy told him he couldn't have the car tonight.

I stand firm and let the dripping water make its shivers over me. Eddie is scurrying back and forth across the field like he is trying to free himself from a strangle. He's waving his arms and pulling himself forward from things I can't see. Bucky follows him and his angel hands are held out trying to touch Eddie.

"You're lost, Eddie," I yell, my voice cracking, "lost as they come," but he's not listening. He's running wild through thistle bushes.

A Stranger Comes

Mama is screaming. Daddy tries to take hold of her, but she only wants to wander from one room to another, her howls worse than the wolves we sometimes hear at night.

"Lydia, Lydia," Daddy says. He walks behind her. He's tall but faint, the way a shadow can be. Bucky twists himself into the kitchen couch and sobs, his body tight and his face skin red.

I run outside and dart back and forth on the lawn, shaking my fingers, which have the feel of fire. Each breath is a jerk out of me. From the side of my eye, I see Marilyn. She comes out of her house and runs toward me. The sun has gone down. The sky is a pink sea behind her. She doesn't look both ways before she crosses the road like we're supposed to, but makes a straight beeline for me. When she is close enough for me to feel her breath against my face, she stops still and holds her eyes and lips in an O.

"My brother Eddie is dead," I whisper, proud for a second because Marilyn only has a sick person at her house.

"I know," she says. "He burnt up in your daddy's car."

"He burnt up?"

Marilyn doesn't answer me, but turns and runs straight back to her house, her legs thin and light like a spider's.

The word *burnt* drops down inside of me. I fall down on the night grass. Mama's howling plugs my ears and makes me think of drowning. I whisper, "Mama, Mama."

I have a wide awake dream that Eddie is hiding behind the house. He comes around to pick me up off the grass. I was just fooling, he says. I'm not mad at him anymore. I wrap my arms around his neck. I kiss his pouting lips over and over, the way I always want to.

I suck in specks of dirt, storing them in my mouth the way squirrels do their nuts. I like the way the dirt grinds against my teeth. It makes me know I'm still alive.

I was on the verandah listening for the whipporwill when the Mounties' car came into our yard. I was thinking about what Daddy said to me once when I told him that I didn't have anything to do.

"Go dig yourself a hole," he said. "Dig and dig and when you get to the other side of the earth, there will be a little China girl waiting for you. She'll have slanted eyes and you won't be able to understand one word she says, but you'll probably figure out a way to talk to each other."

I was remembering that and trying to figure out just what the China girl and I would say when I looked up and saw the Mounties' car. Daddy came right out of the house. He had been reading his paper and it made a kite when he stepped outside. He stopped and folded it under his arm before he walked to the driveway. He pulled at one ear and said, "What'd he do now?"

The Mountie got out and put his hand on Daddy's shoulder. I saw Daddy's chest cave in. Mama came out on the verandah. "What is it?" she asked, shy. "What's wrong?"

Daddy turned. "It's not good, Lydia," he said.

Mama's breath turned to crying before she even heard what Daddy had to say. I stayed in the verandah chair, listening to Daddy's low and heavy words rumble. They made their way like an earthquake and they were just as powerful, because when they touched my mama's face, it just filled with cracks.

I think back further to when everything was okay. I search for a loophole to let me out of what has happened. It was a pretty good day up until now. Eddie got braces on his crooked teeth and then he got his driver's license. Daddy took Bucky and me for a walk in the woods and the names of trees rolled from his mouth, *elm maple poplar beech pine fir,* each one as crisp and clean as the forest floor. Mama made shepherd's pie for supper and we had it with ripe tomato pickles and canned peaches for dessert.

It gets pitch dark. The preacher comes with his hat in his hand. Dr. Pearly comes right behind him, his black bag just the right size for a sitting cat. Mama's crying has lost all its shape and it's flowing fast like the creek rapids do in the spring. I stand up on the verandah and Dr. Pearly touches my head and pulls it into his black pants. They smell of mothballs. He doesn't say what he always says to me and every other kid from the Upper Valley: *I was the first one to see you when you came into the world.* Instead, he just wraps my head in his hand and lets his wooly pants soak up my eyes.

Having two big men in our house makes Bucky and me settle down. We sit on the couch and lace our fingers together, white and tight and looking like giant crochet work. Mama is at the sink window, her body aflutter and Daddy is there with her, aflutter too.

"Sit down for a minute, Lydia," Dr. Pearly says. He touches Mama's shoulder and she gives into him the same as I did. She droops into the chair. Dr. Pearly rubs her arm with wet cotton, then he lifts a long needle from his sitting cat bag. Mama drools while she cries. Bucky's fingers tighten stiff in mine. Mama doesn't seem to notice the needle going in. She just takes it like she is too tired to fight. When it comes out, it pulls her words with it. "It's all my fault," she breathes. "I was always trying to make him perfect."

"Don't be thinking that now," Dr. Pearly says.

In the morning, Sister's man drops her off and she walks in behind three lady neighbors who are carrying cakes and casseroles. She lets her babies down. Her red eyes are a match for Mama's. Only one neighbor doesn't cry when Sister and Mama melt into each other. Mama is still wearing yesterday's dress wrinkled from her sleeping in it. Daddy takes Sister in his arms and she snorts against his chest. The sound of it makes the company turn and walk from our house. Their heads are down like Bucky's is when we play war and he surrenders.

"We have to go and pick out the casket," Daddy tells Sister and it makes a rise in all of us. The sound of echoing voices comes up in our kitchen. I can't help but wonder if the angels are crying with us the way the Bible says they do.

After Mama and Daddy drive away with Mr. Morris, Sister and her babies sit with Bucky and me on the kitchen couch. Without Mama and Daddy and Eddie, we are in a ghost house. I look at all the food on the counter and I wonder why the neighbors brought it. No one wants to eat. "Did you get any sleep last night?" Sister asks.

"We slept with Mama and Daddy," Bucky says.

I remember myself, my head on Mama's pillow, watching her open staring eyes. I touched her warm beaded neck. My hand wasn't nearly as soft as her neck. "Are you all right, Mama?" I asked.

"No," she said. "The needle made my body go to sleep and now nothing can get out. I'm numb all over."

Then the whipporwill started up. *Whip-por-will, whip-por-will,* until I had to get up and go into Eddie's room to look out the window. The moon was out making the yard gray. I looked for the whipporwill in the trees, but there was no sign of him. Then I began to look for my brother. *Whip-por-will, whip-por-will.* "Couldn't You bring Eddie back, Jesus?" I asked, searching the lawn in case Eddie lay out there somewhere, waiting. I listened and looked down the road. "Couldn't You?"

When I turned around, Eddie's silver comb on his dresser was covered with the moonlight. I picked it up and I could see his smudged fingerprints on it. I put them to my nose to smell. I rubbed it like I would the Savior's feet and the prints faded beneath my fingers. In the comb's teeth, there was one black hair. I picked it out.

When I got back to the bed, Mama and Daddy were awake with their backs to each other. Bucky was stretched out straight in between them, sleeping with his mouth open. Mama and Daddy were curled up like pictures of babies in their mamas' stomachs. For a minute, I forgot about Eddie being dead and I thought what was making everybody lie so strange might have something to do with the twisted sheets or the gray light beaming in from outside. I waited for someone to move so there would be room for me.

Now I'm sitting in the kitchen with Bucky and Sister, feeling achy. When a knock comes on the door, I follow Sister to see who it is. We both smooth down the fronts of our wrinkled dresses. A man with a black mustache half-smiles at us. He speaks English with the leftovers of another language. He might be from China, except his eyes aren't slanted. "Are you Eddie's mother?" he says, soft.

Sister lowers her eyes. "I'm his sister."

The man puts his face close to the screen. "I'm sorry," he says. He takes a shaky breath. "It was my parked road grader that he hit."

Sister's back stiffens like she is getting ready to take a punch, then she slouches like the punch came and took her breath away. Her tears drop down. One warm one lands on my arm.

"I'm very sorry." The man opens up the screen door and takes Sister in his arms. She rests her head on the curve of his shoulder. His blue jeans are low on his hips and when he stands back from Sister, I notice his eagle belt buckle. I study its golden shape. I learned in school that the eagle is the sign of freedom, but I've never seen one. I also learned that eagles lay eggs with shells so thin that they sometimes break under the weight of the mama bird.

"Come in," Sister says, wiping her face with a holey tissue.

The man follows her into the kitchen and I go with them. Bucky is lying on the couch. The babies are on the floor beside him. When they see the stranger they say, *DaDa DaDa DaDa*. He smiles at them and goes over and puts his hand down for Bucky to shake. Bucky's hands burrow underneath him like wild animals. The stranger's hand hangs in the air, alone.

"Shake hands," Sister says to Bucky.

"No." Bucky turns his face to the wall.

The man looks at Sister. "Are your parents here?"

"No," she says. "They've gone to . . ." She turns and busies herself with the food that the neighbors brought. She piles the plastic containers like building blocks. "They'll be home soon."

The man looks at the ticking clock, then walks out on the verandah. I follow him. He sits down on the step and lights a cigarette.

"Eddie smoked," I say.

"He did?"

"Yep. Want me to prove it?"

Ever since the snow melted, I have been watching that

pack of cigarettes in under the bleeding heart plant, the ones Eddie dropped the day he got out of jail when he was yelling at Sister from his bedroom window. They're the ones that came loose from his shirtsleeve and swirled to the ground like a red and white bird shot dead.

I reach in and lift the pack from under the blooming plant. I lift the top. It's practically full of cigarettes that have faded and gone mushy from the weather. I hold the pack in my palm and let the stranger admire them. "These are his," I say.

"Are you going to save them?" he asks me.

"Mama would kill me," I say.

"Maybe you could hide them." His eyes are soft and dark dark brown.

I hadn't thought about saving them, but I like the idea of it. It's hopeful. I hold them to my chest on my way to the wellhouse where the sun is shining bright. I sit down on the stone step and lift every cigarette from the pack, one by one. I lay them even on the step. They make a fence. Some are wet and break apart but I push them back together. I hold the empty pack and watch while they dry out in the light.

Our driveway has started to fill up with cars. Everyone

that gets out is dressed up and whispering. Mona from up
the road comes and the preacher drives up. My uncle comes
with his wife. She's wearing a big pink sun hat. They all
stop and speak to the stranger who keeps looking down this
way to check on me. I watch him up there on our verandah
greeting everyone and holding the screen door. It makes me
think of heaven. There is supposed to be a man at the gate
ready to meet us.

Mama and Daddy drive in with Mr. Morris. Mama is
in the middle and Daddy is beside her with his arm in a
boomerang out the window. I stuff the cigarettes back in
the pack even though some of them are not dry. Daddy's
brother comes out to meet them and Mama falls into his
arms. The others look down and kick at the dirt. Uncle Neil
leads Mama into the house and it's not long before her wailing starts up again. The stranger walks down and shakes
Daddy's hand and I suppose he tells Daddy what he told
Sister earlier. I worry for a minute that maybe Daddy will
hit him, but everything stays gentle.

Daddy walks toward me. The other men come behind
him in a line. Daddy stops. He looks down before opening
up the wellhouse door. "Better go up to the house," he says.

I stand up. My legs dip because they are full of pins

and needles. I hide the cigarettes behind my back. The stranger is the last one in the line. He reaches down and takes the cigarettes from me. There is already one lit and burning from the side of his mouth. He puts Eddie's pack in his shirt pocket and pats it a few times like he is trying to get his heart going, *thump ka thump*. He winks at me. "I'll save them for you."

Now Mama is on the kitchen couch and Sister is fanning her. All the company has found chairs to sit on while they eat sweets and egg salad sandwiches.

"I don't know if I should have picked the white casket," Mama says. "White is really for babies or a girl."

I look for Sister's babies but they must be napping. I'm the only girl here. Can Mama mean me? I stand very still and hold back my breathing.

"Ssh, Mama," Sister says. Mama starts to cry and her face blotches up. "Eddie is just ashes now."

I squeeze my fingers tight and wish hard that someone would take my feeling from me. My aunt with the pink hat reaches down and brushes my hair from my face. Her fingers are bony. I think of the stranger down in the wellhouse drinking beer with Daddy and his brothers. I picture his eagle belt and wish that it were real. I remember one more thing. When the eagle's egg didn't crack, the mama eagle would pluck feathers from her breast and make a warm spot for the egg to be. I wish that the eagle would come and get me. It would be as easy as picking a petal from a rose.

Voices in the Wind

If I could sleep, it would be a good thing. Ever since Daddy took Mama away to get help for her crying, I lie here in this bed stiff like a mummy. Sister's girl baby is here with me and sleep is wrapped so tight around her that even her toes and fingers are curled.

Daddy took Mama away right after Eddie's funeral. It was the night before they buried him that she started not being herself. She was in the living room with his white casket and she was rubbing it with both hands. It looked like she was trying to make a polish come up. Daddy told me later that she wasn't in her right mind. That was an awful thing to hear about Mama, but hearing her downstairs wrecking Eddie's casket was worse.

We were all in our beds when I saw Daddy go running

down the hallway. His white underwear shorts were baggy on him. Sister went behind him and then me. I didn't know enough not to look. Mama had Daddy's screwdriver and I guess she was trying to get Eddie's casket open. A trembling note came from her, then another and another. I thought of Mama as a solo singer. That might be a funny thing to say, but I know now that sadness can be like that. It can be just like a song.

At the funeral, Eddie's casket was a bad sight, all picked and nicked like crows had been at it. Everyone we knew was there and they were all whispering and the sound they made was a song, too. Daddy said that they were just *speck you lating*. I learned in school what molting was. Speckled baby birds molt and get new feathers. I couldn't make sense of any of it.

After a while, I move away from the warm baby's body and go get in bed with Daddy. I crawl in Mama's spot. It dips down and is shaped like her. I'm too little to really fill it up. Daddy is on his back, snoring. I smell his beer breath and take comfort. Every night, he goes to be with Mama and comes home late. In the morning, while he's eating breakfast, I examine the empty brown bottles under the seat of our new car. It's not really new, just one Daddy bought from the yard of Mr. Morris's garage. There are always two or three dusty cars sitting under the big Shell sign with the prices painted on the windshield. Daddy says they paint them on with a bar of soap. Before Daddy eats his breakfast, he always mixes a raw egg with some tomato juice and swallows it down. He says it makes his head stop pounding. I reach up and rub my hand over his face. First the smooth way then the other way so the whiskers scratch my fingers. My hand fits good into the dent of his cheek. I touch his thin top lip, then push the thick bottom one to change his snoring. I listen for the breaths of everyone in this house. Sister and the babies and Bucky. I wonder what it means for me that Eddie and Mama don't breathe here anymore. Tomorrow, Daddy is taking Bucky and me to see Mama and I can't wait.

I pinch Daddy's nose and his mouth falls open. I keep pinching it until he wakes. He turns on his side and wraps me up in his arms. His bare-naked chest is cool. It smells like the mist under a waterfall. The parts of him that get the sunshine on them smell different. They always smell like wood and that makes me think of Daddy as a little forest. He smacks his lips and says, "Why are you in here, darlin'?"

"I can't sleep, Daddy."

He pulls me in close. I shut my eyes and breathe in the moist green color.

"Just lie still," he says, "and you'll go to sleep." He kisses the top of my head and how strong he is comes right through his lips.

I dream that I am standing on Eddie's grave. It is brown dirt with no new grass yet. I'm just standing there, waiting, when Mama's hand comes up and touches my foot. It's Mama's wedding band hand. Her ring is worn thin like rabbit wire, but her hand is all softness and the smell of flower stems comes from it.

In the morning, Daddy gets out his barber set and puts the stool on the verandah. He calls Bucky and Bucky comes tearing down the stairs in maniac style. I sit on the railing beside the barber set. It's a small box with a see-through plastic apron, long sharp barber scissors, shears to make stubble at the back of your neck, and a round white brush for wiping away the cut hairs when you are finished. I sneak the scissors out sometimes to trim my doll's hair. Bucky hops up on the stool. Sister is in the kitchen feeding her babies breakfast and if I let myself, I can pretend that she is Mama. Daddy starts at the top of Bucky's head and cuts real close to make a brush cut.

"What time you leaving, Daddy?" Sister's words travel out through the black screen just like a radio voice coming through a speaker.

"As soon as we get the kids ready," Daddy says. "Are you sure you don't want to go?"

"I can't, Daddy," Sister says. "I don't want to see Mama after she's had electric shock."

"What's electric shock?" Bucky says.

"Put your head down, Bucky," Daddy says. He plugs the shears into the verandah plug-in. Then he works them up and down Bucky's neck like a lawn mower. They cut even rows of hair and the snippets drop on the verandah floor. The skin around Bucky's head where his hair used to be is milk white. His chin is pressed against the plastic barber apron. "What's electric shock?" he asks again.

Daddy puts the shears back in the box and uses the brush to sweep away the escaped hairs. "It's just something they did to your mama to make her better."

We wear our Sunday clothes, which is the same thing as we wore to Eddie's funeral. I add my white Easter hat with the elastic that goes under my chin plus my white gloves with baby bows on the wrists. I'm careful about washing myself because Mama is very particular about clean children. I put on fresh panties, a new undershirt, and my crinoline slip that makes my dress stick out around me. I haven't had it on since I was little and it's tight on the waistband. I clean my nails with the end of one of Mama's bobby pins, then comb my bangs straight down and press them with spit before putting my hat on.

"Well," Daddy says when he sees me. "Don't you look beautiful." I feel my face blush. I twist my hips. I don't know why, but those two things always go together. Bucky has on a white short-sleeve shirt with his bow tie. We get in the backseat and Sister leans over to check our faces. She holds our chins when she does it. Bucky still has some snipped hairs on his cheeks and Sister rubs them away with her little finger.

We listen to Pastor Myers on the radio while we drive. He's talking about Armageddon, which sounds like one mean place to me. He tells about a woman clothed with the sun who was having a baby. A dragon stood in front of her so it could eat the baby the very second it was born. When we get out on the highway, Daddy stops at a road canteen and gets Bucky and me each a Coca-Cola. My bottle is wet from where they pulled it out of the cooler. I want to try to make it go a long way, but it's hard to keep from drinking it. Before we take off, Daddy pops the cap off a beer with his car key then puts the full bottle between his legs. When there are no cars coming the other way, he takes big gulps. Bucky watches Daddy, then tips his Coca-Cola. The bottle shows green in the sun. He takes in as much as he can then eases the bottle down. His lips smack off the bottle and he lets out a wild burp. We can't help but laugh, even Daddy. "It came up my nose," Bucky chuckles.

Pastor Myers wraps up his sermon and the special singer comes on. Daddy takes a little sip from his beer, then turns the radio up. We're driving along the big river where the air is full of strawberry smell. It's such a beautiful day that lots of people are just out in their yards wandering around. We each roll our windows all the way down. I hold my hat so it doesn't fly off my head and listen to the radio: *Amazing grace, how sweet the sound, that saved a wretch like me! I once was lost, but now am found, was blind, but now I see* . . . Tears roll down Daddy's cheeks. *When we've been there ten thousand years, bright shining as the sun, we've no less days to sing God's praise, than when we first begun.* When the singer is done, Daddy says, "You'd have to be an awful bad man not to love that song."

Bucky and I both finish off our Coca-Colas. Bucky

holds his empty out the window and it makes a high steady noise. I hold mine out and it whines, too: *whooooooooooooooooooooooooooooooooooooooooooooooooooooooooooooooooo*. Daddy goes real fast and people who are out turn and look at our car to see what the moaning is. They almost look scared watching us go by.

I don't blame Sister for not coming to see Mama. We have to go through two locked doors to get to the room where we wait for her. The lawn outside is very beautiful, but inside it is dark like a peach with its velvet outside and its black pit for a middle. My black patent shoes click down the narrow hall behind Daddy and Bucky, making me wish I'd worn my flip-flops.

Bucky and I share a big plastic chair and Daddy sits beside us in a straight chair to wait. There is a woman waiting, too. They bring a man in for her, an old one with white spikes for hair. He sits down and mumbles, "Yes, yes, well you can always tell one of those people. Yes, you can. If you look real close, they got things on them, but you got to look close. From far back, they look just like normal folk." I wonder if he is talking about people who *speck you late*.

I try to move back in the chair, but my sweaty legs stick.

Daddy looks at Bucky and me. He rubs his hands together. "Now your mama may look a little tired, but don't worry, she's going to get better here. And she wants to see you, that's why I brought you."

They bring Mama in a wheelchair with one of her arms tied down. It's the wedding ring arm. Bucky moves back, but I stand up to meet her. Her hair is straight and her eyes have purple underneath them. Her face skin looks like it might be molting. The woman pushing her is big and dressed in white. She pushes Mama in close to us and says, "Just look at this, the whole family is here to see you."

When I look close at Mama, I don't recognize her eyes, so I sit down. My crinoline makes my dress fan up in front of me. Mama looks like someone I shouldn't talk to.

"Lydia," Daddy says, "you're looking better today."

Mama's lips crack open, but they take a long time to smile at him. She wiggles her arm under the rope, but it doesn't come free. She puts her other hand out to Bucky and he drops his head down. His green eyes tick back and forth. I reach out and touch her hand for him and Mama squeezes my white glove so hard that it scares me.

"Not too tight, Lydia," Daddy says. Mama lets up and then her touch is too loose and my hand slips away.

"Was your drive here nice?" she asks.

"We got Coca-Colas," Bucky pipes in, his head still held down shy.

"That's nice," Mama says. "Did Eddie get one, too?"

Bucky and I look at Daddy. We are all held together silent until Daddy stands up. He goes over to the nurse who has been watching us all along and Mama says, "Did he? Did Eddie get one?"

I would like to tell her yes, but I don't believe I should since Eddie is dead. I would like to say, Yes, Mama, we got him a Coca-Cola and barbequed chips and a Sweet Marie bar and some Juicy Fruit gum.

The nurse comes over with Daddy and says, "I think you two little ones better go out and walk around the grounds." Her voice sounds like it's trying to be nice but can't quite manage it. She holds both her hands out. Bucky and I get up and take them. It feels like she's pulling us up out of a deep hole. Mama doesn't watch us go. She's staring out through the window with the bars on it. Daddy stands beside her, rubbing her tied hand. We walk with the nurse but keep our eyes turned on Mama. The nurse scoots us outside, then locks the door behind us. We look back and her snappy wave tells us to keep going.

Bucky and I go over and sit under the shade of a big maple. I take my hat and gloves off. It was a waste that I wore them. We watch the windows until after a while, Daddy pushes Mama's wheelchair to one and she lifts her free hand and waves. We wave back. "Why have they got her hand tied down like that?" Bucky says. "What did she do?"

I look at his pink ear that looks to have grown since he got his brush cut. "She didn't do anything," I say. "They just don't want her to get away."

Mama waves a couple more times, then grabs a bar like she is trying to make it come free. She's saying something, but it's hard to know what it is.

On the way home, Daddy stops at the canteen again and gets Bucky and me each a hot dog and two more pops. We sit at the picnic table beside the red canteen and eat them. Daddy has a cigarette while we eat. "When is Mama coming home?" I ask.

Daddy blows out smoke through his nose. "When she's better."

"When she gets home," Bucky says, "is she gonna have to stay in that wheelchair with her arm tied down?" There is ketchup at the corner of his mouth. It looks like blood.

"Oh, no," Daddy says. "Listen, your mama isn't very

well right now, because she just lost Eddie and it's hard for her to realize it."

"Why?" Bucky says.

Daddy lights another cigarette. "Because the car caught on fire, your mama couldn't see Eddie after he was dead, so she just doesn't believe he is."

I wonder what happened to the Bible woman when the dragon took her baby. She probably didn't even have ashes in her baby's casket. "But we believe it," I say to Daddy. "Why's that?"

Statues

Bucky and I didn't know that Mama was coming home. We thought it was just another day. We stayed across the road with Marilyn Morris and we were standing in the yard with the cow when we saw Daddy pull in our driveway. I was halfway there before I noticed Mama and for a minute, I didn't recognize her because she looked smaller than she used to.

Bucky was running right behind me and yelling, "Mama, Mama." There was a smile in his yelling, but when he saw Mama's bruised face, he ran into the house without even saying hello.

I put my hand in the hot car and Mama kisses my knuckles. My fingernails are dirty so I pull my hand back fast and hide them behind my back. "What is it?" Mama says.

"My fingers aren't clean, Mama," I say and she smiles.

Daddy and I help Mama out of the car. Everyplace I touch on her body has a thin bone jutting out that makes me picture a naked stick woman. Her hand that was tied to the hospital wheelchair has a thin burn all the way around its wrist.

Mama lies down on the kitchen couch and her chest rises up and down. I sit on the floor to be near her. There are bruises around her eyes. They look like they would be soft to the touch. I lean into the sleeve of her dress, which has the smell of the hospital. It smells of boiling vinegar and it takes my breath away.

"Did the electric treatments bruise your eyes, Mama?"

She lifts her head and stares at me. I think she is trying to remember who I am. "Oh, no, dear, they beat me in there."

"Who did, Mama?"

"The nurse did."

I look to see if Daddy is going to say anything about the nurse, but he just goes on making the tea, with his head down. "But why, Mama? Why did the nurse beat you?"

Mama opens her mouth wide and rolls her tongue

back. She points in at the blue veins. I get up on my knees and look. "I don't see nothing, Mama."

Bucky, who has had his face wedged in between the refrigerator and wall comes over and looks in Mama's velvet mouth, too. "What?" he says.

Mama shuts her lips and studies us. She has a sleepy daze in her eyes. "I was hiding my pills under there. I wasn't swallowing them like they wanted me to." She moves her face close to us and whispers, "I thought if I kept swallowing everything they gave to me, I might never get home."

Bucky and I look at each other and then back to Mama. It's hard to think about being without your mother forever.

Daddy comes over. "Here's some tea, Lydia," he says. Bucky and I push ourselves back from Mama and follow the squares on the linoleum floor with our fingers.

Pretty soon, Mama stands up and holds her hands out to steady herself. There is a run up the back of her stocking and if you look at it really close, it's a little ladder, wide and straight enough for something small to climb up. "Now," she says, looking at Daddy, who is having his tea at the table, "I'm going to clean out Eddie's room. There's no use in keeping his things—they won't bring him back to life any more than anything else will."

Bucky runs outside when he hears Mama mention Eddie. The screen door bangs behind him. It's the first time we've heard her say that Eddie is dead. I breathe deep enough to find a sigh. It's not a good sigh of course, but something like a person might have if they'd been sick a long time and the doctor finally told them they had a very weak heart.

"Lydia," Daddy says, "why don't you rest today and do that later in the week?"

Mama holds a finger to her mouth and it is bent near the top. The shape of it makes her seem old. "No, I want to do it now and when I'm finished, I want you to take the children and me on a trip. Just an overnight or a couple of days, that's all, and I'd like to take the train if we could. I haven't been on the train in years."

"We could do that," Daddy says, tapping his cigarette pack quick and steady with his fingertips.

I have a daydream about a train. I'm beside the ocean and it's beginning to get dark and everything, the sky and water and sand, is pink. There is a steam train that runs beside the ocean and it's coming toward me. *Chug, chug, chug*. The night air is warm and wet and the train's lights are making a glow on everything. When it reaches me, I start to run beside it and my legs are as strong as a horse's. The waves are lapping in and I know that I can run forever. There is a voice that comes from behind me and it says, Come back, come back, but I can't stop running with the train.

From Eddie's window, I watch Daddy drive off to work. Mama has already started in on Eddie's things, piling them on the bed in stacks. Part of me wants to be speeding off with Daddy, but another part figures I should stay and look after Mama. She holds up a pair of blue jeans with white pressing seams down the front. "Do you know of anyone who would want these?" she says.

"Maybe Leon up the road could use those, Mama."

"Yes, I suppose he could." Mama folds them against herself. Her body is full of caves now, and even her eyes are round and sinking. Her face has the point of a wolf.

She looks about the room, then to the shelf of old bottles that used to be Eddie's collection. When he was little, he found them in fields along the old fence lines. Daddy said in the old days that was where people threw their garbage and now all that is left is the valuables. I can picture Eddie coming home with his arms full of colored glass.

There are deep blue and brown and clear bottles, but my favorites are the gentle greens.

Mama goes over to the shelf and puts both hands on the edge of it. She starts to pull herself up on the shelf and it gives way. It rips from the wall and the bottles tumble to the floor. Mama doesn't put her hands up to protect her face, but lets the glass fall freely at her. The bottles clatter and chime beside her feet and the noise breaks through my skin in sharp splinters. I hold my hands to my mouth. The dust from Eddie's shelf blows a swirl around Mama. She lets go of the shelf. It hangs loose on the wall, creaking back and forth like time passing. Mama turns her tired face to me. "That's how quickly things can change." I keep my eyes on her. "Remember that," she warns.

One of my favorite bottles has broken its neck in the fall. Mama bends down and picks up a broken piece of glass that has the shape of frowning lips. She wiggles it to catch the sunlight, which is streaming in behind me. She wiggles it very close to her wrist. I suppose that I should say something to stop Mama, but I'm afraid she might press that piece of glass to my skin. Daddy told me that sometimes when a wolf gets caught in a trap, it will chew its own paw off in order to get free.

Outside, the cicadas are buzzing. Bucky and Marilyn laugh while they chase each other around the yard. Mama tosses all the broken glass in a beautiful colored pile. Her eyes are perfectly clear. They are the only living part of her bruised face. The sound of the bottles breaking and the sight of Mama has made my insides pound. I tiptoe to the bed and sit near the edge. My heart beats up into my throat.

Mama comes over to Eddie's dresser and opens the top drawer. She lifts out the white impressions that the dentist made for Eddie's crooked teeth. She holds them tight together and up close to her face. The way she twists and turns her head makes me think she's looking in a mirror. Once, I opened a drawer in Mama's room and there was the head of a doll staring up at me. It had dark hair and blue glass eyes and for a second, I thought that doll's head was me looking back at myself. I shut the drawer up quick and never opened it again. A lunge went through me that time.

Mama drops the white impressions in the tin waste can and they echo. She opens the second drawer and takes out the starched shirts, then piles them beside me on the bed. I get up and go over to the window. I sneak a look at the impressions on the way to make sure they didn't break. They are smiling up at me like the teeth of a skeleton.

"Is there anything you want of Eddie's?" Mama asks me.

"I don't know," I say, even though I would like nothing better than to reach down and rescue his impressions.

"Well, if there is, just let me know, but don't wait because everything in here will soon be gone."

I look out the window and wish for my old mama. The one that put her cool hands on my forehead and the one that got down at the side of my bed and taught me to pray to Jesus. The one that hung all our clothes on the line outside and then carried them in, stiff and dry, and pressed the wrinkles from them with a hot iron. I think of the spider shells that I find hanging in their webs on the verandah. From a distance, they look completely whole, but when you touch them, they crack and crumble because their insides are gone.

Mama falls down on the bed with all of Eddie's things and circles in like a flower after a frost. "He was such a sweet boy," she says.

A breeze comes in and blows the sheer curtain in a veil over my face. I watch Mama through it and whisper, "Who was?"

"Why, Eddie," she says. "Who else would I be talking about?"

"I thought you might be talking about Bucky." I take a deep breath and the curtain floats into my mouth.

Mama turns and looks at me. She narrows her eyes, "Get that curtain off your face. You'll get it dirty."

I push the curtain away and go over and sit on the floor beside Mama. The breeze has come in and is making her hair do the hula around her face. I touch her forehead where there are four thin lines straight across. Her skin is dewy and she looks me over. "I don't know who I am," she says. "Do you?"

I think about it, but I can't find the answer. Mama watches me. I figure she knows that I don't have the answer.

"Do you know who *you* are?" she says.

"Yes," I admit. "I'm a child."

She blinks her eyes, then closes them. "Mama," I dare to say. She opens her eyes. I see they are wet. "Bucky and I'll make you happy."

She looks off at the wall like there might be an old movie playing there, then back to me. "There are no happy people," she says, "just happy times." She closes her eyes and now they are framed in the plum bruises. I smooth her silky eyebrows down with my little finger. "That feels nice," she says.

Tears tingle behind my eyes. I wrap my arms around myself and seal my lips so they can't get out. I bow my head and say a prayer for Mama. Her mouth falls open and everything about her settles down. She is as blank as a picture. I lay my head down beside her hand that has the ring of fire on its wrist. I hold my nose close to it and breathe deep. It's still wrapped in the hospital smell, but somewhere underneath, I think I smell a hint of my old mama.

I wake up with the marks of the bedspread pressed in my face. Marilyn is screaming and I rush to the window. She's hollering at her barn cat, Sailor, who has just run across the road in front of a car. His white and yellow body is still stretched out long and speeding over the Morris's yard. "Sailor," she hollers. "You only got about two lives left." He scurries into the barn where there is a chipped saucer of cow's milk. Mr. Morris always fills it up when he milks Sadie.

I reach down into the wastepaper can to take out Eddie's impressions. They are chalky and make white dust on my hands. I hide them behind my back as I pass by the bed and Mama, who is still asleep. In my bedroom, I examine the impressions and count every tooth, top and bottom. There are thirty-two in all. Touching the front ones makes me feel close to Eddie. I touch my own teeth with my tongue. Mine are crooked, but sharp like Mama's. I shut my eyes and memorize Eddie's teeth with my touch, then wrap them in tissues and hide them under my bed.

Outside, I get Marilyn and Bucky to play a game of statue with me. I give them both a good hard swing and they stop right up and hold their bodies still. My job is to catch the first one who moves and then they will lose and have to be It. The parts that the wind moves don't count, because that's an act of God.

Daddy comes home and I run over to tell him that Mama is sleeping. He nods and sits in the verandah chair to read his paper. I run back to catch Marilyn's arm trembling and make her It. Mr. Morris is mowing his lawn. The sweet smell floats in the air. Mrs. Morris is sitting out in their yard on a chrome kitchen chair, watching him. She has her summer housecoat and slippers on. Things are almost like they used to be.

Bucky gets tired of standing still and says we should play something else. "What?" Marilyn asks.

He hangs his hands in his pockets and looks around to think, then holds one arm straight up in the air and yells, "Heil Hitler." He falls back on the ground and Marilyn and I laugh. It's something we do when we are playing in the creek. We fall back under the water and sometimes I open my eyes and see the blurry bodies of Marilyn and Bucky. They always look whiter under water.

Marilyn and I put our arms up and hold our noses. "Heil Hitler," we holler and fall back on the grass, too. We all get up and do it again, "Heil Hitler, Heil Hitler, Heil Hitler."

All of a sudden, the screen pops out of Eddie's window, falling like a thin black cloud to the ground. Mama holds her head and shoulders out under the window and screams, "STOP IT, STOP IT, STOP IT."

I'm sure Mama has heard us say "Heil Hitler" before. We stand up and watch her. There's old grass stuck to my legs and it tickles, but I don't scratch. Mama doesn't look pretty with her bruised face and messed up hair. She yells, "Don't you know Hitler persecuted the Jews?"

Mr. Morris turns off his mower so now everything is

quiet. Daddy drops his paper and rushes out to look up at Mama. He staggers because he has been sleeping in his chair. "It's all right, Lydia," he says. "They'll stop."

"They'd better," she scolds. "We can't have them saying things like that in the yard." Mama pulls her head in and slams the window shut. The pane rattles.

Daddy comes over to us. "Don't say it anymore. Your mother's nerves are bad and it bothers her."

He heads back toward the verandah and Bucky says soft, "Heil Hitler." He holds his fingers to his mouth and smiles, his eyes round.

Daddy turns to come back toward us. He has a firm face and Marilyn runs home before he reaches us. He puts a hand on each of our heads and bangs them together. A loud cracking sounds. Bucky opens his mouth up wide, but no sound comes out. When it does, it's the sound of a baby. I look up and Mama is standing behind the sheer curtain, watching us. She looks like a ghost. I press my lips together and suck them in. Bucky keeps on wailing.

Daddy walks down to the wellhouse and shuts the door. I guess his nerves are bad, too. I put my arm around Bucky, but he pulls away, mad. It's starting to get dark and the windows in our house are black. I think Mama might still be up there, watching me, so I don't move. I cross my feet and twist a curl in my hair.

Later, I go down to the wellhouse to check on Daddy. I open the door and see him sitting in the corner with his brown beer bottle. "Daddy," I say, "who are those Jews anyway?"

He waves me in so I go sit beside him. He has taken his shoes and socks off and his feet are as white as the moon. I look at his toenails, which are thick with layers. They make me wonder if people have nine lives, too. A layer for every life. I study my fingernails and there are little ridges on them. If I counted the ridges, they might equal my age like the rings inside a tree. Daddy takes a long drink and then says, "The Jews are a whole race of people that a very bad man tried to wipe out."

I have to think about that for a minute. "Are there any left?"

"Oh, yes," Daddy says, holding back a burp.

"If I saw some," I say, "how would I know them?"

Daddy pulls me into his sweaty side. He smells like the taste of salt. "Most you wouldn't know," he says. "But the ones that were persecuted have a number on their arms." He points to his wrist. "A little blue number."

Just the way the word, *persecuted,* pushes out of people's mouths makes me know it's a mean one. I think the nurse persecuted Mama and made the bruises on her face. "What's the number for?" I ask.

There is the soft dripping of water coming from the well under the floor. "I figure now it's just a number to remind them of their suffering," Daddy says.

I picture all those people with their numbers hidden under the cuffs of their shirts and sweaters and blouses. I wonder if the Jew children have numbers, too. Daddy has got his sleeves rolled up so I check his arms, but all I see is skin and black hair.

In the house, Bucky is putting peanut butter on crackers for his supper. "Are you all right?" I ask.

"What's it to you?" he says, twisting his face. I touch my head where we got banged together and there is a sore spot.

Upstairs, I stop at the door to look in at Mama, who is sleeping on top of Eddie's bed again. Her arm is held over her forehead and the moonlight makes it look like white marble. Eddie's things are piled in little mountains around her. Her body is like a river running through them.

119

I watch her and think about all of us. Once, we were all just standing perfect like Eddie's bottles used to. We had no idea what was coming our way. I wonder if that is how the Jews feel. I go to my room and get Eddie's impressions out from under my bed. I count his thirty-two teeth again, then press them to my chest to make little ridges there. I think of marks and numbers. It crosses my mind to go get a pen and make a number on Mama's moonlit wrist. I could make it just above the ring of fire, then she would have something real to show for her suffering. I could do it as easy as not.

Audrey's House

I run up the road, past where the pavement stops to the house that has no screens and long sticky fly-catchers that blow in the wind. "Go to Audrey's and stay there until I come get you," Daddy said.

"But I want to go over and stay at Marilyn's house," I said.

"Bucky is going to Marilyn's house. You know that her mama is sick and can only take one of you."

Daddy sent us away because Mama is not herself. She woke up early while Daddy was still in bed and warm beside her. She called out to me, "Come here, baby girl, come here."

When I got to her room, with two red spots on my legs where my knees had slept together, Mama was smiling a long blue stare. Right at me, she said, "Today Mama is going to kill you. Yes she is. She killed your brother and now she is going to kill you, all right enough."

And Daddy pulled out of his sleep like a horse rising up and pushed me away from their room. "Get dressed. Hurry," he said. "Do it in a hurry."

Audrey's family is still waking up. Her mother, Mona, is in one corner, rinsing off bowls. "Well," Mona says, looking down her nose at me, "why are you up so early?"

I rock back and forth on my gritty flip-flops that are getting too small and I say, "Oh, no reason special. I just wanted to play."

Audrey is on the couch behind the woodstove, twisting her brown hair in her fingers. Her lips are the color of old cherries and they look a little used and sore. Her eyes stay soft on me.

"I have to stay until my daddy comes to get me," I say.

Mona lets out a big breath. "Madness," she says to herself, "is an awful thing." She knows about my mama because we are on the same party line and Mona always listens in to everyone's troubles. Daddy says that she does it because she doesn't have a life of her own.

I'm not usually allowed to play at Audrey's house because Mona talks in tongues at her church on Sunday nights and doesn't keep a clean floor. My mama says, "Why go up there, when your own house is so much better. And besides," she always says, "your friend Marilyn is right across the road just dying for your company."

Audrey and her brother, Leon, both look at me funny. I know it's because they have never seen me stand right here in their house like one of them. I look down at myself. My shirt is buttoned up crooked with two buttons missing. My stomach is empty and dizzy and I wonder if Daddy should have sent me here, seeing that Mama says it is not a fit place.

Mona gives me some cereal and we all sit up at the picnic table in the middle of the floor. It's the chipped red color of a park picnic table and I wonder if their daddy stole it away from some treey field. I don't doubt that he did knowing what Audrey has told me about him, knowing that he chased some expecting girl right out of church with a broom, because she didn't have a husband.

Mona is praying a long prayer about wild minds, but Audrey and Leon start to eat anyway, so I eat with them because food can sometimes help me when I'm worried. When Daddy took Mama away before, I ate a whole roll of bologna and then threw up on the bleeding heart plant beside the front steps. That's why Daddy will not let me stay home alone while he takes her to the hospital upriver. I think of Mama in the hospital with the bars on the windows. When Bucky and I left from visiting her last time, she hung on to the bars and I think she was hollering, "Don't leave me here."

Leon watches me real close while the milk runs down his chin. He has a pack of cigarettes tucked in the top of his jeans so he sits very straight. His bare chest is thin with black hair in the shape of a cross. I can see little brown freckles that look like ants under the hair.

Mona looks down at me through her tiny round glasses. "Was your mama rantin' and ravin' like she did last time?" she says.

"No," I say.

"What did it? What made her that way?" She pushes her glasses up on her nose.

"I don't know," I say. But I do, I know a few things. Like how she still sometimes talks to my dead brother like he's alive and sitting right next to her.

When we finish our cereal, Audrey and I go up in the field behind her house where the purple lupines are. "I have to stay here all day," I say. "I have to stay until my daddy comes to get me."

Audrey is still in her ripped nightie and there is a big pile of ratty hair on the back of her head. She is all dreamy and the sun makes her squint in a half-sleep. "Did you ever do it?" she says.

"Do what?" I say.

"Do it with a boy like big people do."

"I don't think so," I say. "Did you?"

Audrey lies back in the long grass. I can smell old pee on her legs. "I do it with Leon all the time," she says.

"You do?"

"Yea."

"Does it hurt?" I say.

"Not after a while." Audrey makes patches with her fingers and covers her eyes. "I'll get Leon to do it to you if you want."

I can see Leon down by the house teasing the tied dog. He holds a long stick in front of him and makes the dog jump and pull on his rope to get it. When the dog gets close to him, Leon bops him on the head with the stick. I think the dog's head must be swollen from the bops.

"No," I say. "I'm not old enough."

"You're nine," Audrey says. "That's old enough. I did it before I was nine."

"I don't think you're supposed to do it with your brother, Audrey."

Her golden eyebrows frown, then she turns her head to her house, which is a tattered gray box below us. I look out to where a rattling car has passed and a cloud of brown dust hangs over the road like it's magic. I say, "Mama was going to kill me, Audrey," and my eyes sting just a bit, the way they do when you get a needle from a doctor.

"She was? She was gonna kill you dead? I sure do pity you livin' with a mama like that. I do, really, it isn't fair," Audrey says.

She jumps up and prances around, picking all the lupines she can. She drops the spikey green stems down on my lap and we pull the little flowers off and stack them like jewels in front of us. Audrey puts one in her mouth and sucks it. "Mmm, honey," she says.

"Real honey?" I say.

"Well yes, what else would it be?" Audrey scolds me. Her face is twisted against the light and I can see little yellow fuzz around her mouth.

We pile and suck the lupine flowers all day until there is nothing left but a plain old field, and our arm skin has grown pink and tender from the sun. I keep wondering if Bucky is having a good time with Marilyn. I swallow hard because I would feel better if I was with them.

When Audrey's daddy drives up in his truck, we run down to the house. He's all dirty from his work and Audrey and I follow him in the house and sit behind the stove and watch him wash up. He has a grumpy face with warts and he doesn't talk to anyone, just rubs his hands hard with the soap until I think they're going to bleed.

Even when he is all clean and dried off, Mona doesn't fix any supper like my mama would. She's fiddling with the transistor radio looking for the Bible man. Leon is in the corner, tossing the dog's stick up and down in front of him. The light on the outside is more than the light on the inside and I say, "I think I'll go home now." I can see myself doing it. I can see myself walking down the long road in the gray dark that comes before night.

Audrey twists the skirt of her nightie in a ball. "What if your mama kills you?" she whispers.

Everyone looks at me. The night makes them all look pasty and dead. Mona comes over by the woodstove and takes a match from the old jelly jar. She strikes it on the stove and starts the fire inside. A big puff of smoke comes up. She pulls her face back from it, then looks around the stove at me. Her legs are crooked sticks under her dress. Audrey stands up and pulls her nightie out from her bottom and watches her mama.

"You're gonna stay until your daddy comes to get you," Mona says, sharp. Then she looks like she didn't mean to sound so nasty. She looks almost sorry I'd say and she glances down at my shirt and teases me, "Did the devil get your buttons?"

"No devil," I say. "Just lost them."

Audrey's room has a bed and a few boxes. Her clothes are scattered rags in those boxes. There is nothing that looks new. She jumps on her bed and the springs make a screechy noise. "You can stay right here," she says, patting the bed beside her. She reaches down the crack between her bed and the wall and pulls out a long knife. She jumps up, then pushes the crooked door closed and wedges it shut with the blade. "There," she says. "That will keep Leon out."

Audrey pulls back the cover and jumps in. "Sleep in your underwear," she says.

I slide my shorts off and kick them under the bed. My shirt is dirty, but I keep it on anyway. The mattress is all bumpy like anthills underneath us. Audrey and I lie in the dark and listen to the Bible man on the radio in the next room. The crickets are making their song outside. We stare through the window glass to the stars, which are a ton of white spots in the sky. "Planets don't sparkle, do they?" I ask.

"I don't know nothin' about planets," Audrey says.

She squeezes close to me and puts her arm around my neck. She licks my nose with her tongue and smiles just a bit. "Your mama will be okay," she says.

I move down into a worn spot in the mattress and pull the blanket up around my face. It smells like dog hair. I think Audrey's eyes are closed and the black dark is looking right at me. I roll back and forth and listen for Daddy's car and I wish so bad that he would come and get me. I get Mama on my mind and think of her the old way, making supper and singing. Mama is beautiful when she's not sick and she knows how to cook and how to make our food look nice. It makes me hungry just to remember. I can hear the dog rolling in the dirt outside our window, scratching his back and whining. The dark is strong and pushing down on me and I'm afraid to look at it. Audrey wraps her legs around mine and we fall asleep that way, all hot and sweaty.

In the morning, the birds sing outside the window and the sun is a splash of light on our heads. Our blanket is down at the bottom of the bed and a small shake goes over me. "Audrey," I say, "did you open that window?"

She rolls her face out from under her hair and looks at the window. She looks back at me, then reaches down for the blanket. "That Leon," she says, a yellow ring on her lips, "I can't keep him out." She turns her back to me and cries way down deep inside of her, little tiny cries that echo off one another.

I swallow the sleep in my mouth and rub the places where my buttons used to be. There are little piles of white thread all tight on my shirt, all neat and tight with no buttons to hang on to.

A Blue Bike

Two weeks ago, Daddy took Mama back to the hospital and I wish that she was here so I could tell her that Marilyn Morris's boy cat, Sailor, had kittens. That even surprised Mr. Morris who took his hat off and scratched his forehead when he saw them. After a while, he said, "Well, you just never know anything for sure."

The big white and yellow cat was blinking slow while the closed-eyed babies sucked the pink buttons on his belly. Marilyn and I were on our knees beside the babies. Mr. Morris leaned over to examine Sailor closer. "Yes sirree," he said, "either Sailor here has been a girl all along and we never knew or some miracle of God took place and changed him into a baby bearing animal."

"Whoa," Marilyn breathed. "could God do that to a cat?"

"I figure He could if He wanted to," Mr. Morris said.

Daddy comes home and gets supper for Bucky and me. His favorite is fried meat so that's usually what we have with a piece of white baker's bread. Daddy dips his bread in the juice from the meat, but I roll mine into my mouth clean. We are having pork chops and Bucky chews on a piece of fat. Grease leaks out and his lips go glossy. "Daddy, did you go see Mama today?" he says, swallowing down smooth.

Daddy says the same thing he says every night. He swings his head low and keeps his eyes on the flowered tablecloth, then the word "no" comes out of him like a hiccup. Mama had been saying a lot of things that weren't like her, so Daddy took her back to the hospital. Once, she even set my dead brother's place at the table and told him to keep an eye on Bucky and me while we ate. Bucky and I just pretended that Eddie was there.

Every night after supper, Daddy goes down to the wellhouse and drinks his beer. Bucky watches television and I usually go over to Marilyn's to admire the kittens, but tonight I sit out on the verandah and watch the dark come in. My new bike is in front of me leaning against the railing. I'm waiting to get my nerve to talk to Daddy. Marilyn Morris says that I can have one of Sailor's kittens and I would like nothing better. She says if Daddy says yes to one, I might as well take the two yellow ones that she believes to be twins. One boy, one girl. Marilyn always says, "You better take as many as you can because my daddy is going to drown the ones I don't give away."

Daddy just got me a new bike so it's hard to ask for something else. I was using an old one of Eddie's and I kept falling on the crossbar and hurting myself. That's why Daddy said he got me a new one, but I have the feeling that Mama wanted to keep something from happening to Eddie's old bike. She polished it up and put it down in the cellar with her preserves.

When Daddy came home with my new bike, his trunk was opened halfway and tied down with twine. I was standing on the lawn when he drove in. I can't tell you what I was thinking. I was just standing there chewing my thumbnail. Bucky tore into the yard on his bike and did a sideways skid right beside the car. His back wheel hissed in the dirt.

Daddy untied the twine and took my new blue bike out. He waved for me and I ran over. It had no crossbar for me to fall on. "Try it," Daddy said, patting the seat.

I thought how Daddy used to put me on the crossbar of the old bike and ride me around. I'd hold my legs out straight to keep from getting them caught and so Daddy could pedal easy. We'd go way up the road and back. It always felt safe the way his arms came down around me. "We won't be able to ride double anymore," I said. Daddy reached down and touched my head.

Bucky is in the little room laughing at "The Jackie Gleason Show." *One of these days, Alice, Pow, right in the kisser.* I remember Mama's bruised face from the nurse beating her. I wonder if maybe Daddy shouldn't have taken her back there. The sky is letting its stars out. I suppose the way they hang and twinkle is also a miracle. Like a lot of things, there's nothing to explain why they do it. Marilyn Morris says that once a person goes crazy, it's hard for them to ever be the same, but I still cross my fingers and make a wish on Mama. I wonder if I can have more than one, then take my chances and wish for a kitten. I don't wish for the twins because I know a brother and sister might not get along.

On my walk down to the wellhouse, the crickets sing

and the wet grass spits at my legs. I open the door and a sour smell meets me. Daddy is sitting there in his bare feet with his shirtsleeves rolled up. His case of beer is right beside him. There's a load of empties already. The light bulb overhead hangs on a wire. It spills dusty light down where the old well is boarded up and dripping. Daddy is in the shadows. I hold the door and stick my head in. "Daddy," I say, "Marilyn Morris was wondering if I could take one of her kittens before her daddy goes and drowns them all."

He looks at me. Nothing changes on his face. Maybe he didn't hear me. He's as still as a dead man.

I speak up. "I'd take care of a kitten. It wouldn't be any trouble. I could feed it leftovers. Just the ones that we were sure we didn't want anymore. And I wouldn't let it whine at night the way Sailor sometimes does."

I stare in. I know Daddy is smiling because his side gold tooth has picked up the dull light and is shining. He takes a big swig and his lips kiss off the bottle.

"Do you think I could, Daddy? Do you think it would be all right?"

"I guess so," he says. "But it can't go in the house. It'll have to live outdoors." He holds his bottle up and tips its neck toward me, like we're celebrating.

"That's okay," I say. "Sailor lives outdoors. He's old, Daddy, and I don't believe he's ever been inside a house. He just goes in the barn or under our verandah when it rains and he does all right. Marilyn says he doesn't like being caged up." I wait for Daddy to say something, but he stays still. "Sometimes, Sailor goes away for months at a time and no one even knows where he is."

Daddy taps his wedding ring on the bottle.

"Thanks, Daddy," I say, before closing him in fast. "Thanks a lot."

I skip across the road to Marilyn's and look in her kitchen window. There is just the chrome table with its empty chairs, so I run to the barn.

Marilyn is in the corner with her arms wrapped around Sailor. His eyes are wild from being held. "Marilyn," I say, "I can have one."

She looks up at me. Her eyes are red. She stretches her neck and peers around Sailor's head. "One what?"

"One kitten. Daddy says I can have one just as long as it lives outdoors."

Sailor bolts away from Marilyn and leaves a long scratch on her hand. His body skims between my legs and out into the night. Marilyn rubs the scratch, then crosses her arms in a sulk. "You said if you were gonna get one, you'd be here by suppertime."

"I know," I say, "but it took me a while to ask Daddy."

"Well, you shouldn't have taken so long, because the kittens are gone now."

"Gone where?"

Marilyn stands up and wipes herself off. She fixes her eyes on me. "Daddy put them in a sack and took them down to the creek."

I picture their round bodies squirming in the sack. "Well, let's go after him. Let's run down and tell him I can keep one."

"It's too late," Marilyn says. Her words come out with tears. "You should have got here sooner."

"I couldn't, Marilyn. I couldn't get here sooner."

Marilyn's eyes glisten. "Yes you could have. It's your fault."

I figure the only one that can keep Mr. Morris from drowning my kitten is Daddy so I run home for him. He's fast on his feet and could shortcut through the fields and be there before the kittens get completely drowned. And I know he will, if I ask him.

I open the wellhouse door, out of breath, and see

Daddy stretched out on the floor. He's straight on his side, still in the shadows, sniffing. I tiptoe into the circle of light. His brown empties are all around his head like fallen-down bowling pins. He watches my feet. "I didn't want to take her back there," he whispers.

I kneel down beside him. His eyes look like colored glass. I know he's talking about Mama. He lifts his head and looks at me. His face has more wrinkles than I've ever seen before. They are running downward like stitched seams. "I really didn't want to," he says.

"Then why did you, Daddy?"

The dripping well echoes underneath us and Daddy's eyes tick back and forth. "I was afraid she was going to hurt you," he breathes. Daddy's tears drop on the wood floor and leave dark spots. His shirt is drooping around his neck and his collarbones are shaped like the rim of a bucket.

"Would Mama really hurt me?"

"I don't know," Daddy says. "She isn't herself any-more."

He pushes himself up. There is floor dust on the side of his face. He snorts and wipes his nose with the back of his hand, then stands and wobbles. He reaches up and twists the light bulb out, trying not to burn his fingers. There is no switch. When it's off, his hand falls down. I stand and take it in mine. His fingertips are warm and I imagine lightning shooting through them. "You saved me," I whisper in the dark.

"Oh, no, I didn't," Daddy blurts out. We stand still for a minute over the dripping well, then I pull his hand and he walks behind me. I open the door and lead him outside. It's completely night now. Daddy is walking drunk, but his grip is tight. His shadow comes down around me like a blanket.

Mr. Morris is going up his driveway and his walk is lit by their outside light. His back is curved and the empty sack is bunched up and bulging from his fist.

"I decided not to get myself a kitten," I say.

Daddy swallows back a burp. "Why not?"

"I don't know," I say, looking up at the sky. "I figured I didn't really need one right now. I've got my whole life to get a cat." The stars are even brighter than before. I wonder if Mama can see them from her hospital window. I pick a big sparkling one and hope that she's looking at it, too. I figure if she is, that would be another miracle.

"It's probably just as well," Daddy says.

I stop to look back at him. He stops and sways. Our arms make a bridge between us. "Really?"

"Well, they have a way of disappearing." He looks up and his Adam's apple is bobbing. "The bad thing, though, is that you usually outlive them."

I don't know if Daddy is talking about kittens or miracles. I drop my head and he squeezes my fingers snug. The night has made Daddy's feet look gray. I trace the shape of them with my eyes. There are little bumps on top of each toe and I figure his shoes have done that. I figure that's why he left them in the wellhouse.

I lead Daddy over to the verandah to look at my bike. I pull it from the railing and pat the seat. "Sit here," I say.

He raises his eyebrows to question me.

"Sit."

I put my hands on the handlebars and straddle the pedals. Daddy sits on the seat and I push off. He grabs my waist tight and we wobble back and forth. I keep going, though, and head up the road. I know if I can just get us to a certain point, I'll be able to turn around and coast back.

Good Intentions

I stand with Marilyn at the barn door while her daddy squeezes the big cow's pink teats and squirts warm milk in our faces. It drips down our cheeks and we lick it with our tongues, eager to get every bit. We giggle and squint at the taste. A drop lands on my upper arm. Marilyn's tongue, which feels like the outside of a strawberry, steals it away. It's not like the milk at home sitting coolly bottled in the fridge. It is straight from the mother cow, unpasteurized, and so it feels somehow both dangerous and holy.

"That's all," her daddy says. His big hands have dark oil stains in the cracks. We watch them squeeze and pull, squeeze and pull and listen to the steady stream of milk hitting the tin pail in echoey squirts. Mr. Morris milks Sadie with rhythm. The barn is their old shed and it is small and the inside is dark and cool like a cellar. The warm sun comes down behind our backs and makes a path of light over the old straw that has been laid out for Sadie to sleep on. "You better go look after your mama," Mr. Morris tells Marilyn. His eyes are the color of pennies lost at the side of a road.

Marilyn tugs on my arm and I follow her. Near the corner of the shed, flies buzz in the manure pile, which smells a little sweet baking in the heat. We make a curve around it so our shoes don't get dirty. We walk in a straight line from there to the Morris's house and I stop for a minute to admire the new purple trim on the windows. It reminds me of lilacs.

Inside, the house is quiet and airless. We climb up the narrow stairs to where Marilyn's mama is lying weak and sick in her bed. Her room smells like the inside of an old wooden box. Mrs. Morris has been sick a long time now. She is sound asleep with her eyes shut up as tight as trap-doors. There is a small breeze coming in the window and it lifts the white sheet off her chest and her skin is the color of tiny onions.

Mrs. Morris knows that she is going to die soon and that's why she had Mr. Morris put new trim on the house. Yesterday, while Marilyn was spoon-feeding her some warm oatmeal, she said, "We want all the people that come to the funeral to know we are a family that takes care of things."

Marilyn wiped at the corners of her mama's lips. "Oh, Mama, everybody knows we take care of things. Everybody."

I was sitting at the foot of Mrs. Morris's bed and the mattress felt like soft mounds of lawn underneath me. I heard my voice come up out of my chest before I knew that I would speak and it had the sound of low rumbling in it. "You're talking like you don't want to live no more, Mrs. Morris."

She put her thin hand up to stop the last spoonful of oatmeal from being pushed into her mouth and her hand was more bones than skin. "I've been in this bed a long time," she said to me. "I need a change."

Up until then, I had high hopes about Mrs. Morris getting better. I thought if she got better, Marilyn and I could plan a huge party, maybe even pay a circus to set up for a day. When I told Marilyn my idea, she said, "Geez, don't be wasting your time on wishes like that. You know as well as I do that she's not gonna get better."

Marilyn bothers me when she talks like that. Everything is black and white with her. She says that she only wishes for things that she knows can come true. Her biggest wish right now is that someday Sadie will let her climb up on her back so she can ride her around the yard. "It won't be any different than riding a horse," Marilyn says. "Just safer because old Sadie will be a lot slower."

Marilyn and I watch the breeze lift the sheet and make her mama naked on top. We stare hard at her sagging chest. Her nipples are like acorns. I think I'm getting a chest of my own now, it feels hot and swollen under my dress. I don't want breasts. I try not to look at them. In the bathtub, I keep my undershirt on. If Mama catches me, she fusses. She says that's what Catholic nuns do.

Marilyn twirls her fingers through her short hair. When Mrs. Morris had a little bit of energy last week, she gave Marilyn a Toni and the smell of Marilyn's hair makes the air bitter. I believe Mrs. Morris left the Toni on too long because Marilyn's black hair has gone all frizzy. It's twisted into little knots that Marilyn says no comb will fit through. With her fingers still messing in her hair, she goes over to the bed and tucks the fluttering sheet in under her mama's bony shoulder.

She checks her mama's head for fever, but Mrs. Morris doesn't stir. Her sleeping is real deep. Marilyn says that is death working its way into her mama. She says each sleep will get longer and longer until there's no more waking up. Her mama told her this last week. Marilyn looks down at the night table where there's a glass of water with bubbles in the bottom, a Bible, two bottles of pills, and a small tapestry sewing basket. If Mrs. Morris feels better, she plans to adjust the sides of her funeral dress. Marilyn wipes at the dust on the night table and then makes the letter *M* with her littlest finger.

We hear her daddy come in and put the milk pail in the kitchen. "Marilyn," he hollers from the bottom of the stairs. "Is your mama all right?"

"Yes," she whispers. "She's sleeping."

The word "sleeping" makes Mr. Morris clear his throat. He climbs up the stairs and each step is a solid thud like his boots are cement blocks. He stops at the top and takes a breath, then walks into the room. There are deep lines on each side of his mouth. He bends down over Mrs. Morris. His body looks brittle like an old tree that never grew a big trunk. He puts his ear near her mouth and listens, then kisses her forehead. "I'm going back to work," he says. "When she wakes up, go down and get her some of that fresh milk."

Marilyn looks up at him and her eyes are as dark as the curls on her head. "Don't worry, Daddy, I will."

Mr. Morris touches Marilyn's curls when he walks by and she drops her eyes and smiles. It's the kind of smile that has a bigger one right behind it.

When she hears her daddy's truck start up, Marilyn opens up her mama's dresser drawer. It's full of starched white hankies folded into little squares and the smell of them freshens the room. Marilyn takes out the tube of red lipstick that lies like a long bullet at the front of the drawer. She paints her lips and then mine. The lipstick is very thick feeling on my lips. We stretch our necks and examine ourselves in the mirror. "Your lips are prettier than mine," I say to Marilyn.

She laughs. The orangey red color makes her little teeth look like corn niblets. She takes a tissue and dots her lips then rubs the color on her cheeks for rouge, which is what my mama does when she's getting ready to go to church or grocery shopping. "Yes," she says admiring herself, "but your hair is nicer."

She tosses the stained tissue on the dresser and reaches for a brooch that is full of green shiny stones. She takes my dress collar and pins it on. The collar sags from the weight. "I better not wear this, Marilyn. It's your mama's."

"Oh, yes," she says. "Wear it. It looks nice on your dress. It just matches." She takes a long string of pearls for herself and drops them over her head like they are a blessing. Marilyn always wants everyone to look nice, which is why she plans to be a hairdresser when she grows up. Not only does she want people to look nice, but she wants them to feel good, too. When they took Sadie's calf away from her, the cow's insides went as dry as dust and Mr. Morris said he was going to get rid of her if she didn't give milk soon. One night, Marilyn and I went into the barn to pat Sadie, but she wouldn't look at us, so Marilyn took her shirt off and massaged Sadie's head with it. Don't ask me why she did that. It looked like she was dusting the cow's head. Sadie looked down at the barn's floor for a long time, then after a while she looked up and blinked at Marilyn. Sadie's eyes were glassy black and I couldn't say for sure, but she looked like she was crying. She stuck her long pale tongue out and licked Marilyn's bare belly. Marilyn's face opened right up like it was light itself and she took Sadie's collar and walked her out of the barn to where the night was.

147

"What if someone sees you?" I whispered, following along. "You've got no top on."

"That doesn't matter," she said. "That's not what matters."

I walked to the side of the barn and stood in the shadow that the moon made, to watch them. I think Marilyn was hoping to ride Sadie that night, but they just walked around in the fields, under the big moon. The fireflies lit up where they walked and made Marilyn's skin look like a doll's. Marilyn's chest has not started to grow. It's still hollow like mine was last year and the moonlight danced against it. I got to thinking how the moon makes some things grow and it made me scared for her. My mama always says that if you took a chair and sat out in the garden overnight, you could actually see the tomatoes fill out, because they are part of the nightshade family. I thought of Marilyn and Sadie that way while I watched them. I thought of them as being part of some special family. It was a nice thing to see, a cow and a girl moving as if they were floating, but after a while Mr. Morris looked out from Mrs. Morris's window and caught Marilyn. "Marilyn Morris," he hollered. "Get in here."

Marilyn's head turned in slow motion toward the

house and then back to Sadie. She didn't answer him or stop walking. When Mr. Morris came out the door, his belt was off and snapping between his hands. I ran home as fast as I could.

The next day, Marilyn said he beat her hard for being naked outdoors. There were belt marks still on her legs, but she said she didn't care. She said Sadie had gone back to milking and that was all that mattered.

We open up the closet and look at the funeral dress. It's beige lace and has clear plastic wrapped around it. Even though Mrs. Morris ordered the dress new from the Sears catalog, it looks ancient hanging there, like something you'd see in a museum. "Isn't it pretty?" Marilyn says.

"Yes," I say, thinking what a shame it will be to bury it. Marilyn kicks off her shoes and slips her feet into a pair of her mama's high heels. They are creamy white with the toes out. She stands up straight in them and her round knees knock together. "I'm going to keep everything in this closet for when I'm big," she says. "Mama said I could."

"That's kind of spooky," I say.

Marilyn reaches in and slides her fingers back and forth over the clothes like they are piano keys. "There's nothing spooky about that," she says. "This is my mama's stuff."

We look back at Mrs. Morris and she tilts her chin up as if she is getting ready to catch a raindrop on her tongue. "I think she's waking up."

"Watch her," Marilyn says before running downstairs, the high-heeled shoes flopping and making an echo on each step.

Every day, we watch Mrs. Morris like this and sometimes it makes me wish that when my mama gets sick, she could stay home so I could look after her myself. If she could stay home instead of going to the hospital, I would know just what to do for her, because Marilyn has taught me. I would get her fresh cow's milk and damp cloths for her head. I would find extra pillows and blankets and I would file her long fingernails while she slept. And on Saturdays, I would roll her hair in pink spongy curlers so she could look her best on the Lord's Day.

I go over beside Mrs. Morris and watch her face. Her bones are just beneath her thin skin. The shape of them makes her cheeks look like glass balls. Her hair is the same color as the straw on the barn's floor and her eyelashes can only be seen if she blinks her eyes. "Mrs. Morris," I say. "Is there anything you want?"

She doesn't move or answer me. I look at her chest

and watch for it to lift and lower under the white sheet. After a while, I see it go and it looks slow and sweet like a sleeping kitten's.

When Marilyn comes back up, she has a clean glass and the pail of milk with her. She's walking crooked in the high heels and the milk slops from side to side and makes white dots on her bare legs. Her pearls swing like they're meant to keep time. Marilyn puts the pail on the windowsill and I go over and stand beside her. There is a fly in the center of the milk, sloshing around. Its wings are flapping like crazy. "Did Mama say anything?" Marilyn asks.

"Not yet."

Looking at her mama, Marilyn tilts her own round face. "I think she's sicker today."

"Oh no she isn't, Marilyn. She's just tired." I look out the window and across the road to my house. Mama is hanging clothes on the line and Sister's babies twist and turn under her feet, their small hands reaching up to touch her. Mama used to be shaped like the fat angel pictures in my Bible storybook, but since Eddie died, she's losing her shape. I look back to Marilyn, who has started combing her mama's hair, and I remember what Mrs. Morris told us a long time ago. She said mothers were like churches. She said, "You go to them to find out the difference between right and wrong, but the rest is up to you. You're on your own after that."

Marilyn looks very contented and I feel an invisible thread going from my heart to hers. "What are we going to do when your mama dies?" I ask.

Marilyn rubs her mama's soft hair down flat on the pillow and her hands look like feathers. "Mama says we shouldn't think about that. That everything will work out just fine."

"But I do think about it. What are we going to do? What if she dies when we're here?"

Marilyn puts the comb on the night table and reaches for the white cloth that's draped over the headboard. She folds it crossways and puts it on her mama's forehead.

"We'll call Daddy at the service station, just like we're supposed to."

"Then what? After she's not here anymore, what will we do then?"

"When she's gone," Marilyn says, "we'll look after your mama."

"But my mama can't stay home when she gets sick. She needs a special place to help her stop crying."

Marilyn leans in and admires her mama's sleeping face. "You never know what might happen the next time. Maybe she won't be so bad."

I look back to the clothesline. It's lined with Daddy's work pants and the shape of him is still in them. Mama and the babies have gone back in and the pants look helpless in the way they droop. I look down at the fly in the milk. Its wings have stopped flapping so I reach in and pick it out, then flick it on the windowsill where it shines blue in the sunlight. I hold my fingers to the breeze and let them dry.

Mrs. Morris moves in the bed and opens her sleepy eyes. Her eyelashes flutter. The white cloth on her head makes her look like a bandaged soldier. "I heard singing," she says. "Were you singing?"

Marilyn looks down and smiles. When her mama is awake, Marilyn's smile is wide and toothy like a movie star's. "No, Mama, we weren't singing."

"I'm so hot," Mrs. Morris says, her eyes dewy like they've been staring into a very strong wind. "I feel like my whole body is on fire."

"It's a hot day," Marilyn says. "Do you want some fresh milk?"

"No." Mrs. Morris closes her eyes, her voice almost gone. "Just dampen my cloth."

Marilyn takes the cloth from her mama's head and passes it over the bed to me. "Dip it in the milk," she whispers.

I reach out and take it. "Really?"

"Yes," she says. "It will cool her off. Haven't you ever heard of a milk bath? It's supposed to make your skin young-like."

I touch my face where Mr. Morris sprayed the milk from Sadie earlier and the skin is tight and cool. I drop the cloth in and watch it sink to the bottom. It looks like a white bird drowning. I let it stay there a long time before reaching in and wringing it out.

When I turn back, Mrs. Morris has gone to sleep. I get the feeling that sleeping is like falling into a big hole for her. It's easy to slip in, but every time she wants to lift herself out, it gets harder. Marilyn has pulled the sheet back and Mrs. Morris is naked. She's blowing on her mama's face to cool her. I step closer to look at her mama, who is as long as the bed. I have never seen complete nakedness before. Her skin has a tinge of mauvey pink to it and I believe if I looked closer, I could see through to her insides. The hair between her legs looks thick and soft and golden. Marilyn catches me looking and says, "That's where life begins."

I pass her the damp cloth and she pats her mama's face with it, circling her eyes and mouth. "Before we're born, we live inside our mamas' stomachs."

"I know that," I say.

"I know you know that," Marilyn scolds me. "But did you ever really think about living in there?" She puts the cloth on her mama's belly button and drops of milk run down over Mrs. Morris's hips, which rise up and look like smooth carved wood under her skin.

"Yes," I say, "I've thought about it. I even dream about being back in my mama sometimes."

Marilyn's eyes sparkle. I know that what I have said is exactly the kind of thing she likes to think about and so I tell her more. "When I have been over here all day with you and your mama and I'm real tired, I dream about being back in my mama's stomach."

Marilyn pats the little dip above Mrs. Morris's belly button and fixes her shiny eyes on me. "What's it like?"

I wipe at my face and the red lipstick comes off on my fingers and for a second I think that I'm bleeding. Then I see that it's lipstick that has filled in the tiny cracks in my fingertips. "Being back inside my mama is like taking the train," I say. "You sway back and forth, but you feel happy. It's warm like the conductor has the heat on high, and the very, very best part is that it's just the two of you and you are safe in there with her."

Marilyn looks at me hard and I know by the crease running up and down the center of her forehead that she is thinking about what I've said. She stands up and walks toward the window, almost in a daze, dragging her mama's high heels across the floorboards. "I've never been on a train," Marilyn says dreamy-like. "Is it that nice?"

"Oh, yes," I say, even though when I stop to remember the day my family took the train to visit Sister and her babies, a heaviness comes up and parks itself inside of me. All afternoon, we watched the houses and trees slip by and I remember passing a baseball field and a dozen or more young boys came into view. Daddy pressed his nose to the train window and watched them. They were in white suits with navy blue stripes and the spectators were behind third base. When the field had passed, Daddy's eyes dropped, but he kept his nose pressed to the window for a long time and the sides of his mouth fell down. I think if Daddy'd had the power, he would have stopped that train and watched those boys play ball until the whole game was over.

Marilyn brings the milk pail over and puts it down beside the bed. "It's a funny dream," she smirks. "Why would anyone really want to be back inside their mama? I'm not the least bit interested in that. I wanna go the other way. I want all the things in that closet to fit me." She waves her hand toward the closed closet.

A piece of the plastic that covers Mrs. Morris's funeral dress is caught in the door and the shape of it looks like the see-through wings of the fly on the windowsill.

"But when those things fit you, Marilyn, your mama is gonna be dead."

Marilyn dips the cloth in the milk and wrings it out. She begins to wash her mama's sagging chest. "I know," she whispers and her voice cracks.

She circles each of her mama's breasts, then rubs the cloth up and down the center of her chest where there is a flat bone. The milk drips from the cloth and makes a silky cover over Mrs. Morris's body. Marilyn stops when she hears my mama calling me.

I go over beside the window and bend down, pressing my face to the screen. "I'll be right home," I holler.

Sadie is out in front of the house, grazing in the ditch near the road. She stops to look at my mama. I try to remember before I was born, but the first thing that comes back to me is the sound of birds on the roof outside my window and the slats of my crib making a shadow over my face.

Marilyn begins to hum and keeps making her mama's smooth body wet with the milk. Mrs. Morris is still and it seems like all of the breathing on the bed is coming from Marilyn. Marilyn is humming, "London Bridge is falling down." I look back and the babies hang from my mama like cubs. They pull at her shoulders and hair, but she stands with her feet solid on the ground and the breeze makes dry dust roll around her feet. Bucky is standing beside her, anxious for me to come home to play with him. Mama's tummy is round under her dress and it's sticking out like there might be something new starting inside of her. I study her real close and decide that maybe she's just stretched from having her four kids. I wonder how small a baby would have to be to fit back in.

"If I were you, I wouldn't go," Marilyn says.

I look down at the green brooch on my collar and

think about sneaking it home with me. I touch the stones and they're sharp near the edge. "You wouldn't?" I say.

"No, I'd stay right here and keep on doing what you're doing."

I think about it. Once, when I was playing with the babies in the yard, I looked up and saw Mama in a bedroom window. She was waving and I tried to make the babies look up and wave back to her, but their eyes didn't follow my pointing finger. Instead, their round sweet heads turned one way and then the other, their faces held in a frown at the sun. Mama moved from the window and all afternoon, I watched for her to come back, but she didn't. I kept thinking how it was too late for the babies to catch sight of her.

Mama hollers for me again.

"I better go," I say.

Marilyn is doing her mama's feet now. She lifts each one off the bed and swirls the damp milk cloth around it. Mrs. Morris's feet are stiff like boards. I unfasten the brooch. The weight of it feels perfect in my hand. It has the weight of an egg. I put it on the bed beside Mrs. Morris and its color is bright like a dozen green eyes looking back at me.

"You can keep it if you stay a little longer," Marilyn says. "Mama wouldn't mind."

She pulls the sheet up over Mrs. Morris's body and tucks it under her chin. Marilyn's lips are still covered in the red lipstick and she keeps pressing them together. She cups her pearls in her hand and shakes them and they sound like water rushing over tiny stones. "I'm gonna keep these," she says.

"I can't stay," I say. "Just put the brooch back in the drawer and I'll wear it when I come to visit."

"No way," Marilyn says. "You either stay or you can't ever see it again."

Mama hollers one more time and Marilyn looks at me. There is real sternness in Mama's voice like she might be planning to come get me. I look toward the window and then back to Marilyn.

"Go then, baby," she says, her voice higher than usual and her brown eyes snapping. "Go home to Mommy so she can hold you."

"I'll come back later," I say, but Marilyn won't even look at me.

"Don't bother," she says and then starts to chant,

swinging her head and scrunching her face up like a newborn's. "*BabyBabyBaby / BabyBabyBaby.*"

I stand still and watch her. "Don't be like that, Marilyn," I say.

She stops and makes her lips pout. "Why can't you stay?"

I look down at Mrs. Morris and think of my dead brother. He's buried not that far from here and whenever I go to see his grave marker, the ground over him settles under my feet. "I don't want to know any more dead people," I say.

Tears come up out of Marilyn and her brown eyes float in the clear water they make. "Do you think I want to know a dead person?"

"I thought you weren't afraid of your mama dying."

Marilyn rubs at both eyes with her fingers and then plants her hands on her hips. "Well, I am," she says, staring hard at me.

It scares me to know that about Marilyn and I wipe all the lipstick from my lips with the back of my shaky hand. There are tears inside of me and they are starting to come up. I think they're the kind you might get sitting on a train, watching things pass by. I run down the narrow stairs, leaving the closed box smell of Mrs. Morris's room behind and when I open the door, the new air makes me dizzy. "I'm coming," I holler, but when I lift my eyes to see Mama, she's gone. She has given up on me and gone back inside with Bucky and the babies.

Paper Bruises

It's Sunday and Mama and Daddy's bedroom door is closed. Bucky and I tiptoe quiet past it. Bucky's rubber soles squeak on the shiny floor. We've been downstairs playing doctor. I'm always the nurse who takes appointments and keeps the people in the waiting room quiet and Bucky is the doctor with his operating tools laid out like weapons on the couch. We know that we should only knock on Mama and Daddy's door if it is an emergency and we are sure to remember, because it has been a long time since they have gone in broad daylight and shut themselves up.

Bucky plops himself down on my bed while I look at my nose in the dresser mirror. The sun has given me freckles that I wish I could rub off. We both still have our church clothes on. Bucky pulls his bow tie out and lets it snap back at his neck. It's a convenient one with a rubber band that just stretches over his head, but it's always sideways at the mouth of his white collar. I take a pen and play dot to dot with my freckles. The ink goes on smooth and the shape that comes out is a crooked star. Bucky watches me with his hands behind his head and his body stretched out lazy. His lips are bleached white from the sun. "You're crazy," he says.

"Am not," I say, even though sometimes I wonder if I might be. Lately, my dreams wake me up at night. I'm always running in them, trying to get away from something I can't even see. Once in a while, my legs won't move. In the dream, my eyes stretch bigger and bigger, but no other part of me moves.

Our house is good and quiet without Sister and her babies. She left this morning before church because her man has been calling every night, anxious for her to get home. She has been here helping since Mama came home from the hospital, the day before they found Mrs. Morris sleeping dead in her bed. It was a good thing Sister was here, because Mama wanted cooking to take over to the Morris's and she wasn't able to do it herself. She was tired from the hospital that Marilyn Morris says is called an *a-side-lum*.

"What are Mama and Daddy doing in there so long?" Bucky sighs.

"They're doing *it*." I say.

"Doing what?"

"You know."

Bucky sticks his bottom lip out sulky and tilts his head to one side.

"You know, kissing and stuff."

"What stuff?"

"You know."

Bucky sneers at me.

I look back to the mirror, leaning into it. I blow my breath on the mirror to make my face blur. "Audrey, up the road, does *it* with her brother."

"Does what?" Bucky's voice sounds afraid.

I look at his round red face, then shake my head, disgusted. "Don't you know how babies get invented?"

"Yes," he growls. "Everybody knows that." He stands up and studies the stars on my nose. His fingers lock on his hips like gates. "You look really stupid."

I push him back on the bed and jump on top of him. He kicks and punches. I squeeze his wrists and hold them down tight. I kiss him on his lips. "Yuk," he spits. I kiss him again. "I'm telling," he squeals.

"Telling what?" I say. "That I held you down and kissed you? There's nothing wrong with that. You're my brother."

He bolts his stomach up and I bounce in the air like I'm riding a bull. He grits his teeth. "I am not your brother. Get off me."

I loosen my grip and let him sit up. "Why'd you say that?"

"What?"

"That you're not my brother?"

Bucky sits up and looks down the hallway at Mama and Daddy's closed door. There's a crack of sunlight streaming out under the bottom of it. He steadies his elbow on his knee and leans into the palm of his hand. He taps his cheeks with his fat fingers and lets out a big sigh. "How long is it going to take them?"

"It could take all afternoon," I say, "and maybe some nighttime, too."

His eyes come to the edge and stare at me, then he

rolls them back in his head and lets his eyelids flutter. "Why?" he says. "Why does it have to take them so long?"

"Just relax, Bucky." I'm happy to let Mama and Daddy stay in there as long as they want. I figure it's a good way to keep things from changing.

I study Bucky's freckled face. I think we're enough alike to be twins.

"You are so my brother," I say.

Mama opens up her door and we race toward her. We trip and stumble over a basket of folded white laundry in the hallway. Lots of panties and a bra tumble out. Mama is wrapped in a patchwork quilt and she holds one hand out to stop us. "Slow down," she smiles. Her chin is high and the bones beneath her neck catch the sunlight.

Bucky wraps his arms around Mama's waist and squeezes her. "Not too hard, Bucky," she says. "I have to go to the bathroom."

Daddy has one arm behind his head and he's smoking a cigarette. Their room is so hot and sticky that the purple flowered wallpaper seems to float. Whenever I say "purple," Mama says, "Lavender, say 'lavender.'"

I run around to get in Mama's spot. When I lift the

sheet, it balloons up in the air and I get a glimpse of Daddy naked. He is pink brown and my eyes catch on his center where there is a dark nest, and things resting. I pull the sheet down fast around my chin and look straight ahead at their closet that has no door. Everything in it is neat.

Bucky stands over Daddy. "Blow some smoke rings," he begs.

Daddy takes a big drag and blows a straight line, then three perfect circles. They come out small and grow bigger. When they are almost out of Bucky's reach, he twirls his finger in their center to break them. Daddy does it again and I watch his round-held lips while the circles float from his mouth. His bottom lip has tiny cracks in it. "Good one," Bucky says.

Daddy grins, then blows a stream of circles and they hold our attention steady. When I dream that I'm trying to run, sometimes I have Daddy's legs. I'm the size I am now on top, but when I look down my legs are his, big with long shadows along the muscles, but they won't move. They feel real, but they have no more life to them than a carving.

Mama comes with her hair combed and pinned at the back. She watches Daddy. "Don't teach them to do that."

"It's just a game, Lydia."

"Games are what teach them," Mama says. She stops to look at herself in the dresser mirror, posing like she's facing a stranger. There's a candle on her dresser with a book of matches beside it in case there's a thunderstorm and the power goes out. We always sit in the car when the lightning gets bad, because Daddy says the rubber tires will keep us all grounded. We've never once used the candle to light our way.

Daddy reaches up and butts his cigarette in the ashtray on the night table. A twist of smoke snakes up from it. I get up and give Mama back her spot in the bed. She sits down with her quilt held snug, watching me. The skin around her armpits is wrinkled, but the rest of her is smooth and soft looking. "What's on your nose?"

I touch my nose. "I drew a star, Mama."

She looks at me closer. "You only drew four points," she says. "A star has five."

"Are you sure?"

She looks out to the high hay behind our house. "Yes," she says, "I'm sure. Every night at that hospital, I stood at my window and watched the stars. I practically have the heavens memorized."

"You did, Mama? You watched the stars?"

"Yes," she says. "They shift in the sky every night. One night, the Milky Way would be right over my head and then the next night, I'd have trouble spotting it. Some nights, I couldn't find it at all."

Daddy reaches up and pulls her down beside him.

Mama swallows. "The Star of the East is my favorite. My land, it's a bright star."

"Is that the one they used to find Jesus?" I ask.

"Yes, that's the one the wise men followed."

Daddy wraps Mama in the sheet. The back of her head fits in the rounded part of his shoulder as perfect as dough in a plate. Her face is like white cloth beside his. The sheet makes a valley between them. When Mama was in the hospital, I couldn't remember what she looked like. I had a clear picture of her body and legs and arms, but I couldn't remember her face. As much as I tried, it wouldn't come back to me. Once, I almost asked Daddy if he could remember Mama's face, but then I thought it might make him feel bad. I could dream her face at night, but in the day it was just a mystery.

"Mama," Bucky says, "can I take my bow tie off?" He snaps it at his neck.

"Of course," she says, looking his way. "Why are you still wearing it, anyway?"

He lifts it over his head and throws it on the sheet at Mama's feet. "Yahoo," he yells, taking off downstairs.

"Bucky," Daddy hollers. "Be respectful of the Morris's, they just had a death over there." There is still smoke hovering over Mama and Daddy's bed.

Sister said Mrs. Morris looked just beautiful laid out in her lace dress from Sears. I didn't go to look at her. Sister said I should. She said if you touch the hand of the dead they won't haunt you. I guess Marilyn stayed right beside her mama's casket and even occasionally fixed her hair and added extra blush to her cheeks. I couldn't imagine doing that to my mother. "Was she crying over her mama?" I asked Sister.

"Not that I noticed," Sister said. "Everybody knew Mrs. Morris was going to die. Even Marilyn knew that."

"But she was still scared of losing her mama," I told Sister. "Knowing didn't keep her from being scared."

Before things changed here, whenever I had a bad dream, I got in bed with Mama and Daddy, on Daddy's side. One night I came loose from Daddy's grip and fell on the floor. The next day, my face was bruised and Mama scolded Daddy for letting me fall. I hadn't seen the bruises, but all of a sudden, my face started to hurt. Daddy reached down to touch my face and the black from my bruises came off in his hand. "Lydia," Daddy said, "she must have rolled on my newspaper that was on the floor. It's ink on her face, not bruises." Even when Daddy said the bruises weren't real, my face still hurt. I guess just the thought made them real to me.

Mama sneaks her toes out from under the covers and touches me on the hand. "You knocked the laundry basket over," she says. "Better go and pick things up."

It takes me a minute to remember what she is talking about.

I look at Daddy's eyes, then at hers. They both look sleepy. "You can change, too," she says. "If you want to."

I look down at my dress, then at my legs, which are as straight and thin as new trees. "I can?"

Before I leave, I look out the window to the swaying hay. Marilyn and Bucky are down there playing. Their tracks are like a maze through the high hay. They have tracked out a big circle and they look to be playing doctor. Marilyn has her arm held out and I think Bucky is giving her a needle with a stalk. It's probably something for *nerves*. Dark clouds have come up and are rolling all around the ridge. I wonder if we might have to all sit in the car later.

While Mama and Daddy sleep, I pick up the laundry. I fold Mama's panties into little squares and admire a girdle with round rubber snaps. Everything smells like outdoor air. I sneak Mama's bra into my room and close the door. Mama calls it a *brassiere,* which I think is a beautiful word. It's white with three hooks at the back and adjustable straps. I take off my dress and toss it on the bed, then put Mama's *brassiere* on the way she does. First, she hooks it in front of her, then she twists it around. In the mirror, it hangs like heavy armor and doesn't cover my breasts' place at all. It's closer to my belly than my chest. I twist it around and tie a big knot where the hooks are, then twirl it back and adjust the straps until it lines up just right. The location is good, but the cups are too big for me. Mama's breasts are big.

I open my door and grab two pair of Mama's panties. Daddy is snoring, but I don't hear Mama. She may be staring out the window again. I put a panty in each cup and they fill me out nicely, because they're high-risers. Marilyn Morris says that even when she's old she is going to wear bikini panties. From the front, I'm wrinkled, but when I turn sideways, I look quite natural. I remember Daddy's dark nest with its sleeping parts. If that's the look of all husbands, I'm not sure I want one. Marilyn says I worry too much about the future.

A Private Place to Be

It might be that we are going to the lake because of the heat that's gotten into everything. Even the flowers that I've been watching all summer have drooped over and withered, their stems empty and their heads all dull from the sun burning their edges brown. Maybe it's because Bucky and I like the water and we are always begging our daddy to take us on down to the lake and let us go for a dip to cool ourselves, but I expect that's not the reason. Daddy hates the water; even the creek that runs near our house where Mama taught both Bucky and me to swim bothers him. He says he hates to just sit around while everyone else swims, but Mama says it's because he got a good scare once and almost drowned. I expect that Mama is the reason he is bringing us today. We could say, Mama, we are going to walk way down in the field and play on the railroad tracks and watch for the train and she would just look right on through us as if our skin and bones were invisible. Her sadness feels worse today, like a new sadness has come along and piled on top of the old one.

The back of my dress sticks to the car seat and even with all the windows down and our hair blowing around our heads wild, we don't cool off. The wind is as hot as the air. Bucky is holding a red wooden apple in his hands and the heat in him is making fingerprints all over it, fingerprints that I think he should polish away with the inside of his plaid shirt.

The traffic is late summer traffic and there is a string of cars and campers as far as we can see—a giant tin snake moves in the shimmer above the hot road and we're part of it in our own big car. Daddy hangs over the steering wheel and his sweat is in the shape of a pear on his white shirt. "It's not a good day to go anywhere," he says and I don't suppose that it is, but we are going and Bucky and I are glad.

When we start up a big hill, Daddy passes a blue car towing a camper and a loud popping noise blows right into us like someone is trying to shoot us. Mama screams out and then she sobs. Her hands are red and shaky around her face and her voice trails through the car. Daddy looks the other way at the river that's running by the road and then squints his eyes at the white houses on the other side. Bucky and I lift our heads so we can look back at the camper.

"It blew a tire," Daddy says. "It just blew a tire, Lydia." Mama keeps on sobbing. I reach up and touch her hair, which is crazy from the wind. I rub my hand over and over her curly ends, but it doesn't help. I don't think she even feels me behind her.

Daddy parks behind our rich uncle's cottage because they're not here and it's a private place to be. Of course, Bucky and I would rather be over on the main beach where all the other kids are, but we don't complain because we want to keep everything going smooth. Our uncle's cottage is painted deep red and there's a built-in barbeque in the backyard. When we get out, there isn't even a breeze to welcome us.

"I bet there's a key under their step, Daddy," Bucky says. "I bet we could dig around and find it and then we'd be able to go inside."

"No, we're not going in," Daddy says. "It's not our place. We are just going to park here and use their dock."

Mama gets the quilt out of the backseat and lays it by the side of the cottage where there is shade and Bucky and I go around front to the water. The heat is a soft wall in front of us. We take our clothes off and lay them on the dock gently like we are still in them. We have our bathing suits on underneath. Mine is a red and yellow one-piece and Bucky's trunks are also red with a white lining. I keep my arms folded over my chest. The dock is hot and dry on our feet and we are careful not to step on any splinters. Daddy comes down behind us and takes his white hanky from his back pocket and shakes it. He wipes his shiny skin, which is the color of peanuts. He squints in the sunlight and his forehead wrinkles. "You must be awful hot in those long pants, Daddy," I say.

"Long pants are cooler," he says and puts his hands on his hips and kicks his knees forward to relax.

Bucky is skinny and the part of him where his summer shirt has been is white. Mama always says he has a farmer's tan. "I could swim clear across this lake," he says. "And back."

He hops on the hot dock then sits down and sticks his

curly big toe in the water. "It's warm, Daddy. The water is warm, just like bathwater. And look"—he points back by the shore where the water is lapping over brown pebbles— "look at the clams."

"They're mussels," Daddy says.

Mama walks down and her face is blushed pink from crying. She sits on the dock and puts her feet in with Bucky's. All of the color has gone out of her eyes. Daddy watches her. He has his hanky rolled up like an egg in his hand. I step down to the shore and wade in. I walk crooked on the rocks. Bucky plops in the water and lets his whole body slide under. Mama watches him and Daddy grins. The edge of Mama's dress is getting wet, but she doesn't care. She just stares into the lake with her clear eyes. Bucky swims underwater and then jumps up with one hand in the air. His shiny dark hair is pressed down flat on his head. "Not too far out, Bucky," Mama says. We all look at her for a second and figure maybe she isn't going to be sad anymore.

Bucky swims back toward us. I'm standing in the water up to my belly and he wraps himself around me. "Don't," I laugh. "Bucky, you'll knock me over."

Daddy has his back to us. He's staring at my uncle's cottage. I think he probably would like a cottage of his own so he could go inside on this hot day and cool off. The sun is beating down on Mama's head and there are white hairs picking up the light, white hairs that I've never seen before. Bucky and I twirl around in the water, hanging on to each other and already his fingers are beginning to shrivel. I'm careful not to let his chest touch mine.

"It's hot," Mama says and lifts her feet from the water. She walks up toward the cottage, leaving wet footprints on the wooden dock that the sun sucks up fast. We watch Daddy follow her. He stops for a minute and looks back at us. "Don't go in over your waist," he says and with the sound of his voice, we hear kids shouting way down the beach and smell the steamed hot dogs that are sold at the Lake Canteen. We take all those things in and watch Daddy until he's out of sight.

"What's wrong with Mama?" I say.

Bucky tightens himself around me. His legs are bony. He looks at me. The lake water is dripping down his face in tears. His eyes won't look at mine. "Bucky," I say. "You know, don't you?"

He nods his head, then says, "She peed a baby down the toilet."

"No," I say.

"Yes, she did. I was in there with her when she did it. She peed it down and she looked at it for a long time."

"Did you see it?"

"No."

"Was it dead?"

Bucky's bottom lip comes out and his eyes pick up all the glossy green from the lake. "It must have been," he says. "She flushed it."

For a minute, he hangs tight around me, then he lets go and swims over to the dock where his red apple is sitting in the sun. I know he's telling the truth. Sometimes, when we want to be alone with our mama, we go into the bathroom with her. There is a wicker clothes hamper by the window. I've sat on it a million times, just looking out the window and down to the field, waiting. I can imagine Bucky sitting there, watching Mama.

"But why did she tell you that?" I ask.

Bucky stops for a minute and looks to the dark windows in the big cottage, his face scrunched in the white light. "I guess she couldn't help but. She felt bad, you know?" He blinks his eyes. "Just about as bad as when Eddie got killed."

We stay very still and then Bucky holds the apple out

to me and it sits like a gift in his hand. "Let's dive for the apple," he says. "Toss it for me."

I move toward him and take it, but I'm still thinking about the baby. I'm worried that it might float back up someday when I'm sitting on the toilet. What will I do then? Will I tell someone or will I just flush it back down? I look to where Mama and Daddy have gone, but there is only the red cottage and a tall pine tree that's as still as a statue. "I hope they don't eat all the sandwiches," I say.

"They won't." Bucky is standing with his hands together in a prayer, ready to dive in. I look up at the hot sun and throw the apple right up toward its blinding brightness. It comes down near me and floats on the water. Bucky jumps in and swims along the bottom. His face is blurry coming to the surface and more than ever, he looks like a dolphin. His hand comes up and wraps around the apple and then his face breaks through with his mouth open. He breathes deep. "I'll throw it for you," he says, gulping air.

"I don't want to go under," I say.

He smiles and his front teeth catch the reflection of the lake and for a minute, they look like they're moving in his head. A motorboat starts up on the other side and roars out into the middle of the lake. "I bet they're water-skiing," Bucky says.

I dip down to my neck to cool off and then go and lift myself up on the dock. Bucky swims over and passes me the apple. I twirl it around in my hands and study the stem, which is a little sliver of brown leather. I toss it out and Bucky dives in. The apple sits on top of the water like a red marker. I look back to the cottage, but there is still no sign of Mama and Daddy. Bucky comes up and shouts, "Record time." He runs back, pushing the water with his hands like he's trying to part a path.

"Bucky," I say, "look at all the mussels here on the bottom." He wipes at his eyes, which are getting red, and goes under for some shells. He comes up and splashes a few on the dock beside me. "They're empty," he says. He puts the apple beside them. "Toss it again. Farther this time."

"Bucky, I'm getting hot."

"Get in," he says.

"No, splash me," I say and he begins to splash with both hands. I'm laughing and I want to yell Stop, but my throat is dried up from the sun. I grab the red apple and toss it way out to get rid of Bucky's teasing. He stops to smile at me and then dives in. I watch him wiggle under the water toward the apple floating straight out in front of me. The sun is hot underneath my skin and I rub my wet hands over my arms to cool them. The mussel shells have dried already and their color is becoming purple in the white light.

I watch for Bucky, but he doesn't come up. The apple is still rocking back and forth on the water from the waves that the motorboat has made. I stand up and look for him. I walk back and forth on the dock and search the lake with my eyes. "Bucky," I say, expecting him to come up any minute. My eyes sting from the sun. I rub them and look out again. The motorboat is doing big wide circles, sounding like a chain saw.

When I run up to the cottage and around to the side where I know the quilt is, Mama and Daddy are stretched out on the blanket holding each other. Mama is crying like she already knows something is wrong. I step back by the cottage, afraid to tell them any more bad news. I look out to the water, but Bucky still hasn't come up. I keep hoping he'll come up and make everything that is about to happen different. I look back and watch Mama and Daddy. Daddy's arms are big and solid around her. "Mama," I say. "Mama, Bucky didn't come up."

Both of them sit up and look toward me with their mouths wide. I run back to the dock and they are right behind me, running over the pine needles. "Where did you see him last?" Daddy says.

I point out and my hand shakes in front of me. "Going straight out to the apple."

Mama and Daddy look out to find the apple and then they both jump into the water and the lake wraps around each of them.

"Right where you're going," I say. "He should be right there." Mama grabs the apple and they both go under and for a while they have all disappeared into the lake. She comes up way past where the apple used to be and her blouse is tight, showing her nakedness underneath. She stretches her arms out over the water like a white bird being chased. Daddy comes up and they look at each other and dive back in. The lake is a shimmering sheet over my family.

They come up farther out and Daddy is holding Bucky in his arms. He runs in with Bucky and Mama runs beside them, her arms paddling at the water. Bucky's face is blue under his dark hair. "Why did he go out past the apple?" I say, but no one answers me.

Daddy lays Bucky on the dock beside my feet and the empty mussel shells, then rushes up on the dock and flips Bucky on his stomach. Mama climbs up too and the whole dock is wet and dripping. They make a big shadow over me. Daddy pushes on Bucky's back, but nothing happens. He pushes hard and leaves his fingerprints on Bucky's skin. He looks like he's kneading bread. We have all watched the commercials on how to save a drowning person, only on television, little boys always drown in a pool. Daddy turns Bucky over and looks at his face, then he puts his lips over Bucky's and starts to blow. I wonder how many times in Bucky's life someone is going to need to blow breath into him. Daddy blows two or three times and stops to watch for Bucky's chest to rise. He blows again and Bucky throws up.

When he is finished being sick, Daddy sits him up. He wipes at the corners of Bucky's lips. Bucky squints his eyes and stretches his mouth in wide open-mouthed cries like Sister's babies do. We watch him and listen. For a minute, the sounds from the beach go hushed and the sun sizzles down on us. Daddy pulls Bucky into him and Mama takes a big breath and sits down to rest herself on the edge of the dock. Her chest is rising up and down fast. I sit on Bucky's laid-out clothes and cry. "I did it," I whisper, "I threw the apple," but all anyone hears is Bucky's crying.

"You can stop crying now, Bucky. Everything is going to be all right." Daddy takes a towel and dries Bucky off, then looks over at me and winks. He picks up Bucky in his arms. Mama stands up with them. She puts her hand on Bucky's wet foot that's just hanging in the air. I stand up and look at him. His blueness is all gone. His hair has made a part in the middle of his head. Daddy starts up to the cottage with Bucky. Mama and I go with them, the apple in her hand between us like something glued there.

The Goldenrod Field

When I ask Mama if I can go to the old folks' home to visit, she says yes, as long as I walk near the ditch and I'm sure not to stay too long and tire Mrs. Harris. I outline my lips with Mercurochrome before I leave, then sneak out past Mama, who is talking to Bucky about knowing Jesus. She tells him that there will come a time when it will be up to him to get saved. "Now?" Bucky says.

"You'll know," Mama says.

Bucky bites his bottom lip and frowns at Mama. He's not big on guessing games.

Mrs. Harris has a bouquet of goldenrod in a white pitcher on her nightstand. She is propped up on her bed, eating orange Jell-O cubes. It takes her blurry eyes a while to know me. She tells me that one eye is clear blind with cataracts, then says, "I haven't seen you all summer. Where have you been?"

I smooth my hands down over my dress, then go close enough to touch Mrs. Harris's wrinkled and black-dotted hand. The silver spoon wavers in it. "My brother Eddie got killed in a car crash," I say, even though that's not the biggest thing on my mind.

"Oh, I heard that, dear. That must have been a terrible thing for you." She pushes a Jell-O cube on her spoon and feeds it to me. I suck it down whole. Mrs. Harris eats one and then feeds me one until they are gone.

She looks into my eyes. I think all her living years are what gave her cataracts. I think she's looking through a lot of blurry memories while she watches me. A tractor sounds in the distance and I imagine the brown field dust whirling around it. I picture a boy on the back jumping off to pick up the bales of hay, his smooth tanned arms shining in the sun and his eyes squinted to keep the dust out.

"Mrs. Harris," I say, "last week I almost killed Bucky. I almost made him drown in the lake."

She touches her lips. "You did?"

"Yes," I say, feeling even worse now that I know his soul

wasn't saved. I remember the time Marilyn told me about knowing Jesus. We were taking turns on the ratty swing in the tree behind her house. Marilyn said all I had to do was close my eyes and ask Him to take away my sins, so I did. There wasn't anything to it. When I got home, I told Mama that Marilyn saved me and she said, "Marilyn can't save you. Jesus has to."

Mrs. Harris gets up and straightens the crochet doily on her dresser. "How did you almost drown Bucky?" Her voice is light and shaky like her hands.

I sit on her bed and study my fingernails. "I threw a wooden apple out so he could dive for it and I threw it too far. I threw it where it was deep." The words pop out fast.

Mrs. Harris picks up the brush and pulls it through her white straggly hair. Her window is up with no screen and the houseflies buzz in and out. "Why did your brother go out that far?" Mrs. Harris asks.

I breathe deep and take in some of the dry day's heat that is floating in the window. "Because that's where the apple was, Mrs. Harris."

"Oh," she says as if she suddenly remembered some important thing. Her hair is getting very flat from her brushing. "I picked bouquets all summer," she says, watching herself dreamy in the mirror. "Whatever flowers were growing in the yard, I'd pick them and bring them in. When nothing was in bloom, I even brought in a few weeds. I was the only one to see them, so most would say it didn't matter, but after I looked at them for a while, they began to bother me and I didn't keep them very long."

I look at the goldenrod and there are hundreds of little black bugs crawling over it. Mrs. Harris comes back to the bed and stretches out. She folds her hands over her chest and she is so old and wispy that it's easy to imagine her dead. She looks toward the window. "I didn't have a visitor all summer," she breathes.

I bite the side of my thumbnail watching her milky eyes until they look at me. She focuses good this time. "Is Bucky okay?" she asks.

I remember Daddy pulling Bucky from the water and running with him to the dock, where he kneaded his back, then turned him over and blew into his mouth. "Yes," I say, "but I think Mama still blames me."

She comforts her head on the white pillow. "Are you mad at your mama?"

"No," I say. "She's mad at me."

Mrs. Harris tilts her head and smiles nice at me. For a time, we let things hang between us without talking. After a while, she says proud, "I have a new friend."

I wonder if it's someone real or if it's her imagination talking. When Mrs. Harris told me about her husband who lives up in the attic and I told Mama when I got home, she said he had been dead for years.

"A boy," Mrs. Harris says, sitting up. "Not a boyfriend, but a friend who is a boy."

"Really?"

"Yes," she says. "Would you like to meet him?"

I shrug my shoulders.

Mrs. Harris sits up and slips on her old fluffy slippers, then reaches for my hand. She scuffs down the shady hallway of the old folks' home, her slippers two dirty clouds beneath her. A bitter smell floats up from the floor and I imagine a river of bleach running underneath us. There are other people moving around, but they are as slow and quiet as Mrs. Harris. No wonder Mama calls this place heaven's waiting room.

Mrs. Harris opens the door of the last room and takes me in. There's a boy sleeping in a wheelchair. His body is twisted. He has a white T-shirt and a big white diaper on. The rest of him is thin and bare. His knobby fingers meet at the center of his chest like the wounded wings of a bird.

"That's my friend, Arnie," Mrs. Harris says. "You must have heard of him. He's one of the Lewis boys from over on the ridge."

I picture the Lewis house with its peeling paint and its leaning cow barn out back. "What's wrong with him?" I ask.

"Nothing," Mrs. Harris says. "He was born like that." She lets go of my hand and scuffs over to him. I look around the dark room, which only has a tight-made bed and a nightstand with a bouquet of goldenrod. She rubs the boy's face. "Hello," she says. "Hello, Arnie."

His eyes open wide and his crooked hands come up and fly around his face. I do not move.

"Arnie," Mrs. Harris coos, happy that she has made him come to life. He opens his mouth and it's a long wide mouth full of sounds. "Yes," she says. "I know, Arnie. I know what you mean."

Mrs. Harris looks back at me. "Come and touch him," she says. There's drool on his chin.

"I don't want to touch him."

"Why not?" Mrs. Harris asks. "He loves to be touched." She brushes his stringy hair back from his forehead and he moves so much that his wheelchair rattles.

"Mrs. Harris," I say, "he's wearing a diaper."

She looks down at him and up and down his spindly legs. "He needs to wear one."

"He's big," I say. "There's something wrong with a big boy wearing a diaper."

Mrs. Harris looks at me with her blurry eyes and says, "There's something wrong with all of us."

I bite my bottom lip, squint my face, and stare back at her.

"Come over here beside him," she beckons.

I go, but take my time, stopping here and there to swing my hips.

"Just look into his eyes," she says. "They're perfect. And you know what? He's never done anything wrong. He can't."

I bend closer and he watches me. His body and face jerk, but his eyes are brown and warm. "Why can't he do anything wrong?" I ask.

"He's an angel," Mrs. Harris says.

I touch his chin and he jerks, then makes a noise that

sounds like loud laughter trapped inside of him. I jump back and hide my hand. "He's crazy," I say.

She puts her hand on her hip. "You know, there's a woman who works here who says the same thing. She says she's going to take him down to the church some night and get him healed. Healed from what, I ask her."

"Well," I say, "he isn't right."

Mrs. Harris's eyes water. I look away from her, then go and stand beside the flowers on the nightstand. Behind them is a can of air freshener.

"Can't you see the good in him?" Mrs. Harris asks. She pats the boy like a pet and he coos and grunts at her.

"No," I say.

She squints. "Are your eyes open?"

"Yes," I say, "they're opened." ·

Mrs. Harris unlocks the wheelchair and rolls the boy into the hallway. "I'm taking him outside," she sings back. "He loves the sun."

I follow behind and stomp my feet. I came here to talk to Mrs. Harris about almost drowning Bucky and she isn't paying much attention. She has a lot more speed when she is pushing the wheelchair so I have to hurry to keep up. An old man holds the door for her to wheel her new friend outside. He watches me go by and I wonder why Mrs. Harris couldn't be friends with him instead. "Pretty red lips," he says to me.

Mrs. Harris hurries the boy across the gravel driveway to the lawn. In the sunlight, his veins run blue and look like they could be a map to something. There's a circle of rickety lawn chairs with rickety people in them. Most of them sit very still with their mouths dropped wide open. Mrs. Harris races through the circle and I follow close behind. I walk fast and even. I hold my hands out to steady myself like I'm walking a plank. When we get to the other side, I say, "Mrs. Harris, I came down here to tell you something and you haven't even heard me."

"Oh, yes," Mrs. Harris says. "I heard you. You came here to tell me you were mad at your mama."

"No," I say, disgusted. "I came here to tell you I almost drowned Bucky."

Mrs. Harris bounces the boy over the bumpy lawn. "But you said Bucky was all right."

"He is," I yell. "He is all right. But, but, Mama . . ."

She stops and watches my sputtering lips. "Say it," she coaxes. "Your mama . . . your mama what?"

I take the wheelchair from Mrs. Harris and start to run

with the crippled boy. I head down toward the field where the goldenrod is growing. He slaps at himself and hollers deep noises. I look back and Mrs. Harris is scurrying to keep up. Her bent elbows make her hands swish beside her hips. "Run faster," she hollers. "He loves it."

I don't want him to love it. I run down over the hill and rip a path through the goldenrod. The black bugs take flight. Stems and blossoms churn in the wheels while I race him through the lake of flowers. The wheelchair stops short on a rock and the boy flies out. He lands on his side and curls up like a baby.

Mrs. Harris catches up and gets down beside him. His body is twisting and turning. She lifts his head and waits for his eyes to look at hers. "Arnie," she smiles. She catches her wind and laughs. She lies down beside him and giggles. "Oh my goodness, that was wonderful. Wasn't it, Arnie?"

I stand stiff and chew at the side of my thumbnail. I watch Mrs. Harris until she squints up through the sunlight at me. "Don't worry," she says, "he's fine."

I let my held breath go. "How do you know?" I ask.

"I know him." She sits up and rests her hand on her chest. "There's a part of him living right inside me."

I look back at the old folks' home and I can see the

shape of a man in the attic window. It looks like the man who held the door for us when we came outside.

"Help me put Arnie back in the chair," Mrs. Harris says while she's getting up.

She lifts his shoulders and I go for his twisted feet and legs. They wiggle in my hands, but I hang on tight. He turns his head back and forth, sucking in his wet lips, but his eyes watch me. His body is so light that I wonder if he really is an angel.

We lay him in his chair and Mrs. Harris turns it around and starts up the hill. The hill is steep, but Mrs. Harris's stride is strong. She walks sure of herself when she's pushing Arnie. She pants softly. "That was good," she says and breathes deep.

We walk side by side. The hay tractor still putts in the distance. "Did you remember what you wanted to say about your mama?" Mrs. Harris asks.

I wipe a piece of goldenrod from my dress. "No."

"Did you run so fast that you forgot?"

"No," I say. "I just don't want to say it anymore."

I reach out and steady Arnie's head while he goes over the bumps. It is warm and wet under my hand. I wonder if maybe he *could* be my friend. I pant, worn out from my run through the field. We are getting close to the circle of old people. One woman is slumped over sideways and the sun is lighting up her face. I try to picture her as a little girl, but nothing comes to mind. I can see her as someone's mama, though, and it wouldn't really have to be all that long ago.

My Day

Summer is over and tomorrow Bucky and I are going back to school. Today is my tenth birthday and Mama is planning a party. Her apron is tied tight around her waist and she's beating seven-minute frosting for my chocolate cake. When I came downstairs this morning with my hair pinned special at the top of my head, she smiled. "Oh, you look dear," she said, "and you really should, because this is your day."

I reach into the bowl and scoop some white frosting out on my littlest finger. I study its shine.

"It's like seafoam, isn't it?" Mama says.

"Yes," I say, even though I'm not really sure what seafoam is. For the first time, I notice that Mama's smile is shaped just like mine. Our lips make curves at the edges.

"Mama," I say, "why is this the cake you always make for our birthdays?"

"You like it, don't you?"

"Yes, Mama, I love it."

"Well," she says. "My mother always made this kind for me. I guess we tend to bake the cakes our mothers baked."

Bucky is upstairs playing Eddie's electric guitar. He doesn't have the amplifier plugged in so the sound coming down is a weak *ping ping ping*.

I go outside to look at my day. The sun is high and bright and the warmth of it is almost out of reach. The bees buzz around the last summer roses on the bush. The roses are red, fading pink in places. I think how nice it would be to pick Mama a bouquet. I reach in very slow to avoid the thorns. The sweet-smelling flowers come off easy and some of their petals fall and decorate the bush. When I pick the last rose, my hand comes back with a bee stuck to the fatty part of my palm. I try to brush it away, but its stinger goes right in. It hurts me quick and then circles off in a buzz. I holler for Mama. She comes out and her forehead is frowning. "What is it?" she says.

"A bee stung me," I sob, holding my fingers up stiff in the air.

She takes my wrist and leads me into the house. It hurts so bad that I yell. Bucky rips down the stairs and looks at me. "What happened?"

I'm still holding the red rose bouquet in my other hand and the petals have made a path from outdoors. Their thorns stick me, but the pricks from them are nothing compared to the bee sting.

"A bee got her," Mama says. She mixes some baking soda with water and packs it on my sting. My chest lifts up and down and it's hard for me to catch my breath. "There," Mama says. "Try and think of all the fun you're going to have at your birthday lunch. Daddy is coming home and your sister will be here with the babies. I called Marilyn yesterday and she's coming over."

Mama's lips and the sound of her voice trinkling down over me makes me calm. "We're going to set a table up outdoors and have our lunch. It'll be nice," she says. "It'll be a real party."

Mama wraps white gauze all the way around my palm and fingers. She bandages it loose because she knows it will swell. It looks like a white paw. The soda helps the sting. My crying is just sucking noises now.

We hear a car door shut, then Sister's babies *lalala*-ing

in the yard. Mama rushes to the screen door and I go right behind her. The babies are walking on their own and they smile happy at us. "There's the birthday girl," Sister says. She's carrying a big box.

"Guess what, Mama?" Sister says.

"What?"

"I sell Tupperware now." Sister lifts her chin and tosses her hair.

Mama pushes the screen door open for Sister to come in. The babies are following like ducklings. The girl baby has got her arm around the neck of a rag doll and is chewing on a strand of its hair. Mama bends and kisses the girl baby's face and she giggles. Her cheeks are pudgy pink fat.

"Yes, I'm in the Tupperware business," Sister says, "and I'm going to set the whole birthday table with my samples so you can see it." She puts the box on a kitchen chair. "Women are buying Tupperware faster than I can order it."

Sister bends over to admire my birthday cake. "Oh, Mama," she says. "Look at that beautiful cake. You haven't made one like that in ages."

"I know," Mama says. "It's been a long time."

"Sister," I say, holding my hand up. "A bee stung me."

"Ouch," Sister says, planting a kiss on her fingers, then

patting it on my cheek. Her bubble gum pink nails scratch my cheek gently. I have never seen Sister's fingernails painted before.

When Daddy comes home, the fold-out table is set up outside with a red checkered tablecloth and Sister's Tupperware samples. I hold my bandaged hand up for Daddy to see. "Look what happened," I say.

"What did you do?"

Bucky has put the guitar with its amplifier on the verandah. "A bee stung her," he yells out.

"Bucky," I holler. "I wanted to tell Daddy."

Daddy cups my ears with his hands and points my face up toward his. He has the softest eyes of anyone I know. "Is it better now?"

"Yes," I say, "I think it is."

The babies are already at the table, waiting for their lunch. They have Daddy's old ties tied around their waists to hold them in the big chairs. Mama brings out the cake on a Tupperware plate. It has pink and white candles on it with one of the red roses that I picked in the center. Sister comes behind Mama with a tray of potato salad and the hot dogs and buns just the way I like them, steamed.

"Look." Bucky giggles and points to the road. Marilyn is riding her cow, Sadie, into our yard. Sadie lumbers along, chewing her cud and Marilyn rocks back and forth on her back. Her bare white feet point to the ground like a ballerina's. Ever since Marilyn's mama died, she has been working at making Sadie her pet and I guess there isn't any reason why a girl and a cow can't be friends. She rides Sadie right up to the table and the babies' eyes go wide. "Moo," the baby boy says.

Marilyn slides off Sadie's back and looks at me. "I brought Sadie so you can have a ride after your birthday lunch. That's my present to you."

Sadie's tail swishes back and forth and it fans the barn smell around us.

"That was nice of you, Marilyn," Mama says, "but could you put her over on the lawn now? Just until we eat."

Marilyn slaps Sadie's back and then pushes her toward the grass. "Go."

Sadie moves slow, glancing back at us, first one way, then the other.

We sit up at the table and Mama gives thanks to Jesus. The babies fold their hands and squint their eyes. "Bless this food to our needs," Mama says. "And be with us now and always in both sad and happy times, amen."

"'Men, amen," the girl baby says.

"Where'd all these plastic plates come from?" Daddy asks.

"They're my Tupperware samples." Sister lights up. "I'm in my own business now."

"Well, good for you," Daddy says.

Sister grabs a deep green bowl with a clear snap top from her box beside the table. "Just look at this." She lifts the cover off and there's a green plastic spike in the bottom. "It's a lettuce crisper. You just poke that spike through the bottom of your lettuce and it will keep for weeks in the fridge."

"Imagine," Mama says.

Sister's face is pink from the sun. "Isn't it amazing? Isn't it the most amazing thing you've ever seen?"

We are all still with that question when Bucky says, "The most amazing thing I ever seen was the night Eddie died." He chomps a big piece of hot dog with his mouth open.

Daddy lays his fork beside his potato salad and Mama

stops chewing. The perkiness in her lips slacks. "What?" Daddy says. "What was that?"

Bucky gulps and his eyes go wide. He looks at Daddy. "That night when I was sleeping in between you and Mama, there was a big puff of smoke up over the bed. It waited over us a long time, then it floated down to the foot of the bed and its shape changed."

Sister shivers. "What do you mean its shape changed?"

"It took on the shape of a boy."

"It did?" Sister says.

"Yep," Bucky says, nodding his head. "Then it floated off into Mama's closet and disappeared."

"Oh, Bucky," Mama says, "you were just dreaming that."

"No, Mama, I wasn't dreaming because my eyes were open when I saw it, they were wide open." Bucky stretches his eyes to show Mama.

I remember standing at Eddie's window that night and looking for him out in the yard. I knew he was dead, but I kept hoping. "Do you think it was Eddie?" I ask. "Do you think it was Eddie come back?"

Bucky takes another bite of his hot dog and chews. "If

it was, it was him when he was little because the shape that cloud made was no bigger than me."

"Oh, Bucky, you're going to get everyone nervous," Sister says. "We all know that once a person dies they go right to the hereafter."

"But maybe he came back home just before he went," Bucky says. "Maybe it was him trying to say good-bye."

"Maybe it was an angel. I've seen them before," Marilyn Morris says.

A cloud passes and makes a shadow over Mama's face. Daddy's eyes are two blue ponds. I don't know whether to believe Bucky or not. If he is telling the truth, I wish that he could have taken a picture of the boy shape to prove it to us. I remember the story of Shadrach, Meshach, and Abednego that I learned in Sunday school. When they were put into the fiery furnace, they didn't burn. There was someone in there protecting them. We were all on fire with sadness that night. Maybe Eddie came home to protect Mama and Daddy and Bucky. Maybe he was with them, even though he was supposed to be dead.

Mama stares.

"Mama," I say. "Are you all right?"

"Yes," she says. "I'm okay. I was just wondering about Bucky seeing that shape like that." Her voice is caught between a cry and a laugh. She looks at Daddy. "Maybe it's a message to us. Maybe it means he's in heaven."

"My mother's in heaven," Marilyn says. She has a little streak of mustard on her chin.

Mama blinks. "Of course she is, Marilyn."

There are soft footsteps on the driveway and we all hunker down because we have been talking about the unknown. When we turn our heads, we see that Audrey has come down from up the road. Her T-shirt has a hole at the neck and her hands are in fists at her sides. She looks at Mama and her eyes are just like Arnie's at the old folks' home. "My mama says she accidentally picked up the telephone when you were inviting Marilyn to your girl's birthday party." The sun makes Audrey's tangled hair look like it's woven around her head. "She said you must have forgot about me, so she told me to come down anyhow."

We all look at one another.

Daddy gets up and gives Audrey his chair. He fixes a hot dog for her and spoons some potato salad on a clean Tupperware plate. Audrey leans up. "I just want cake," she says, admiring it at the center of the table. She puts her fists in front of me and opens them as slow as a blossom. Small seeds have made marks on her palms and they drop to the table. "Lupine seeds," she says. "Just for you."

I smile at Audrey and touch them. She smiles back then takes two huge bites of salad. I guess she forgot she didn't want any. She swallows without hardly chewing.

Sister clears the table. "The secret of Tupperware," she says, "is the covers. They keep everything sealed tight. That way, nothing gets spoiled."

Mama lifts the cake and puts it down in front of me. The sun has made it lop to one side. Daddy lights the leaning candles, then a cigarette with the same match. The fire is almost on his fingertips when he blows the match out. Sister says Tupperware is the easiest thing in the world to wash and the babies clap their hands.

"Think of a wish," Daddy says to me. "Think of a good one."

I do and keep it secret.

Bucky runs over and turns on the amplifier. He plays "Happy Birthday" and he is very natural with the tune of it. Everyone sings. Their voices all together are holy. I cup my white bandaged paw to my chest and listen, watching each person's lips move gently over the words of the song.

Mama's blue eyes are more beautiful than ever and they look like they want to love me. The babies sing *lalala* and Daddy watches close. It's a good thing to finally be together. I know we are not all of us, but we are what's left.

The Sparrow

Mama has done my hair in ringlets. She does this the first day of school every year even though I think now I might be too old. I slept in pink spongey curlers the night before so my hair would curl. The ringlets are stiff with hair spray and if I hunch just a little, they brush my shoulders and stray hairs come loose and hang down.

I sit straight, looking down at my desk. There are carved names that make a map on its surface. In the corner, near the hole where you keep your water cup, is Eddie's jagged name. It's cut deep and the lines curve.

Mrs. Mackie rings the big brass bell even though we are all in our seats, waiting. She tells us to stand. Some kids put their hands over their hearts to sing "God Save the Queen." I start out with mine like that, then let my fingers drop and follow the rough shape of Eddie's name. I make soft circles over him. When I started school, Eddie was supposed to be in grade seven, but he had only made it to six.

Mrs. Mackie used to hit Eddie. Once, when I was in grade one, Mrs. Mackie was pacing the floor with a heavy book open in her hands. She was teaching the older kids the capital of each province. "New Brunswick," she'd say and then they'd say, "*Fredericton*," in harmony.

"Newfoundland."

"*Saint John's.*"

"Nova Scotia."

"*Halifax.*"

Mrs. Mackie's flowered dress pulled across her wide back. She lifted the book in her hands and slammed it down on Eddie's head. He didn't see it coming. His head jerked to one side and then he collapsed down onto the floor like a building exploding. Once, I saw them blow up an old building on the news. They said it was condemned. The room was quiet except for one gasp from Eddie.

Mrs. Mackie nudged at him with the toe of her square shoe. "You get back in your seat and answer out when I say a province."

Eddie pulled up and gathered himself at his desk. One

side of him was covered in dust. His face was red, but he didn't cry. He folded his arms across his chest and stared up at Mrs. Mackie. I wanted to go be with Eddie, but I was scared the teacher would hit me with the book. I looked away from him instead.

Mrs. Mackie says we will do what we always do on the first day of school. Everyone will stand and say their name, then tell what they did on their summer vacation. She starts with grade one. Mrs. Mackie nods for the girl at the first desk to stand up. Her hair is in ringlets, too. She stands and crosses her legs at the knees like she has to pee. "My name is Nancy Cole and my cousins came up from Minto this summer and the two boy cousins built a tree house out back for me and Sarah Cole to play in. It wasn't up in the tree like it was supposed to be. It was built on the ground."

The other kids laugh and Nancy Cole sits down.

"Next," Mrs. Mackie says.

A boy stands and wraps his little fingers tight around his belt.

"Name," Mrs. Mackie says.

The boy looks at her blank. His hands squeeze his belt tighter.

Mrs. Mackie sniffs. "I can tell you're a Grant just to look at you."

The boy's eyes perk up. I think he hopes that Mrs. Mackie will know his first name, so he won't have to say it out loud in front of everyone.

"I suppose you're too dumb to know your own name."

He crosses his legs and starts to cry. His tears blurt out blubbery.

"Sit down. I doubt if you did anything interesting anyway." There is no rhyme or reason to who Mrs. Mackie picks on, but I've noticed she's particularly hateful to boys.

I put my hand over Eddie's name. One time he got the strap for not answering Mrs. Mackie. Before Mrs. Mackie got to his second hand, Eddie grabbed the strap and ran outside with it. It was winter and he ran out without any coat. I couldn't do my arithmetic for thinking of him out there freezing. All the numbers blurred in front of me. I never figured why after a while Eddie came back in, instead of running home. His face was blue white and his hands were shaking. He walked back to his seat and slumped into it. Mrs. Mackie stared at him over her dark glasses that always slipped down on her shiny nose, but she didn't say

216

anything. Eddie never got hit again until the snow thawed and Mrs. Mackie found the strap out behind the school.

At recess, the grade fours are still introducing themselves. There are mostly girls in grade four and Mrs. Mackie lets them go on and on. My stomach is churning so I ask to go home. As soon as I'm outside, I start to feel better. The sun beams on my head. I watch the graveyard where Eddie is buried until I'm all the way by, then set my eyes on home, which gets bigger the closer I get.

Mama is on her hands and knees, scrubbing the kitchen floor. I start crying when I see her even though I don't feel like it.

"What is it?" she says coming up on her knees and reaching for me.

"Why?" I say. "Why did Mrs. Mackie have to be so mean to Eddie? She used to be mean to him every day."

"You still miss Eddie, don't you?"

"Yes, Mama, I do."

Mama's face nuzzles my neck. Her hair covers my face like moss.

"Was Mrs. Mackie mean to you?" Mama whispers.

"No," I say.

Mama lines her eyes up with mine. There are still those bruises around them. She holds my upper arms tight so my crying won't make me sway. "If she ever says a thing to you or Bucky, you come right home and tell me."

I nod yes.

Mama bends over and picks up her rag. She tosses it in the pail of soapy water and it sinks beneath the suds. "Lola Mackie is never going to pick on one of my children again."

Mama gets up and goes over to the sink to wash her hands. She dries them on her apron, her eyes in a lazy gaze. She takes a slice of bread from the bread box and butters it, then puts jam on top. She puts it on a plate and cuts it into fours like she did when I was little. "You'll feel better after you eat something," she says, pouring me a tall glass of milk.

I take the sweet sandwich in my mouth. "I really don't want to go to school anymore."

Mama sits down beside me. "You're going to school," she says.

I start to cry again. "I can't."

She cups my chin like it is clay to mold. "You hold your head high and you go. Never give up. You keep going because you're someone special. Don't ever, ever let anyone make you feel any other way. Be proud."

"Is it because I'm your girl that I should be proud, Mama?"

"Oh no," Mama smiles. "You're the Lord's girl. He just loaned you to me for safekeeping."

I think about that. Upstairs, in Mama's drawer, there's a locket pin. On one side, it has a picture of Daddy, and on the other side, there's a picture of Sister when she was a baby. I've never seen Mama wear that pin. It's always in the same spot, tucked between two lace hankies. I figure Mama wore the pin when she was younger, but wearing it now after she's had three more kids might not be right. She still keeps it though and I bet sometimes she even opens it up to look.

"Now finish your milk and go back to school."

Outside, near our step, a sparrow has fallen and is lying on its side. I kneel down to get closer and its eye blinks. One wing is spread flat underneath it like a bed. It doesn't move when I put my hand on it, but its eye goes straight and still. I lift it up and the wing comes loose and hangs beneath. I gather the floppy wing up into my hand.

"Mama," I say, waiting at the screen door. "Come here, Mama."

She comes and spreads her fingers on the screen as if to blot something out. She looks at the bird, solemn. "It must have hit a window. Wait and I'll get you something to put it in."

The bird's heart is beating hard.

Mama brings a shoebox lined with an old pink towel. I put the bird in gently and wrap my arms around the box. The sparrow is calmer now. "Mama, I'm going to take it to school with me, all right?"

"Yes, if you want to." She goes away, then comes back with a piece of white bread that she lays beside the bird's feet. "You can break this bread up for it if you think it needs it."

I walk slowly, but I still get to school too fast for my liking. From outside, I hear Marilyn Morris talking about her summer. She is telling how she trained her cow, Sadie, to act like a horse. I open the big door and slip inside. Mrs. Mackie eyes me. "Are you better?"

"Yes I am. I'm better. I found a bird with a broken wing." I go over and show it to her.

She glances in, but the bird doesn't really interest her.

I wonder if it might be a boy. Mrs. Mackie has the eraser end of a pencil in her ear, rolling it around. "Put it beside your desk until lunchtime."

I walk to my desk and all the kids strain their necks to see the sparrow. This is what it must be like when you get married and walk down the aisle. I cover the bird with the towel so it won't be scared. After Marilyn, I'm the next in line to tell about my summer. I put the bird on the floor and tuck the towel back by its neck so I can see its face. There is blood by its beak. I break off a crumb of bread and touch it to the blood. The sparrow doesn't open to take it so I leave it resting on its beak, just in case. If it opens its mouth, the bread will automatically fall in.

"Next," Mrs. Mackie says, tapping her pencil on her desk to get my attention.

I stand. I haven't made anything in my head to say.

"Go ahead," Mrs. Mackie says.

"This summer," I say. "This summer, my brother Eddie got killed."

"Start with your name," Mrs. Mackie says.

"And my mama went to the hospital twice."

"Your name," Mrs. Mackie says, stern.

You hold your head high and you go on . . .

I look down at the sparrow and the crumb of bread is gone. I lift my chin and I can still feel the warmth of Mama's hands there. "My name is Laura," I say. "Laura, Laura, Laura."

The teacher convinces me to leave the sparrow while I go home for lunch. She says the bright sun won't be good for it.

I run all the way home for lunch and I eat it fast. I'm anxious to get back and take care of the sparrow. This time, I'll wash the blood from its beak and give it water. I'll stay with it, always.

Back at school, the box is empty and the pink towel is folded up in the bottom of it. The teacher tells me the bird got better and flew away. I'm not sure that's true, but I can imagine the sparrow with its wing healed and flying. I see that the bad wing is even with the good wing, that he flies straight without wobbling, up toward the sun.

Look for these Algonquin
Front Porch Paperbacks at your local bookstore:

Daughters of Memory by Janis Arnold
ISBN 1-56512-031-0 $9.95

Passing Through by Leon Driskell
ISBN 1-56512-056-6 $8.95

The Cheer Leader by Jill McCorkle
ISBN 1-56512-001-9 $8.95

July 7th by Jill McCorkle
ISBN 1-56512-002-7 $8.95

The Queen of October by Shelley Fraser Mickle
ISBN 1-56512-003-5 $8.95

Music of the Swamp by Lewis Nordan
ISBN 1-56512-016-7 $7.95

The Hat of My Mother by Max Steele
ISBN 1-56512-076-0 $9.95